Migrant Industrial Complex
~ a Tale of Desperate Travelers ~
by
Margaret Fletcher Malone

To Jen,
As the circle is without end,
So is the love I have for you,
my friend, Thanks you for
Sharing your poly-creativity
which so inspires me,
XXXs
Peg Malone 11/27/2022

Migrant Industrial Complex
~ a Tale of Desperate Travelers ~
Margaret Fletcher Malone

ISBN: 978-1-7335008-1-4

Well Being Publishing Company, Oklahoma.
wellbeco@gmail.com

Key Words: Fiction, Adventure, Youth, Hispanics, Our Lady of Guadalupe, Asylum Seekers, Mother and Children Detention Separations, Racism, USCCB, Catholic Charities, Catholic Sisters, Nuns, and Priests, Border Patrol, Border Detention, Spiritual Awakening, Immigrants, "Migrant Industrial Complex."

Cover Art: Anonymous. Painting purchased by Pamela Vestal at a street fair booth featuring arts and crafts by and for Homeless Persons, Tulsa, Oklahoma, Spring, 2018. Author received permission and was given the painting to use in publication.

EPIGRAPHS

"The mass of men leads lives of quiet desperation and go to the grave with the song still in them."
Henry David Thoreau

"Her face tingled with smiling as she *Recognized Me!* and *Filled Me!* with *Being Dearly Loved*! Experiencing *that,* my world was changed, in a twinkling of an eye!"
Margaret Fletcher Malone

DEDICATION

In solidarity with our Migrating Children, Mothers, Fathers, Brothers, Sisters, and Abuelas. Thank you for bringing your enriching presence into the United States. In gratitude to Catholic Charities, Sister Norma Pimentel, M.J., Executive Director of Catholic Charities of the Rio Grande Valley, Asylee Women's Enterprise (A.W.E.), Grannies Respond/Overground Railroad (Catherine Cole, Ama Kennedy, Sharon Kutz-Mellem, Jackie Jolly, Rebecca Vandergrift, Yolanda Sanchez, Bonita Armaro, and many other Volunteers), Angry Tias and Abuelas, All grassroots activists, Ursuline Sister Michele Morek and Dan Stockman (Global Sisters Report in North America); USCCB (United States Catholic Council of Bishops); OKC, OK Catholic Archdiocese canonization workers for Beatified Priest Rev. Stanley Rother, who was martyred in Guatemala; Women's Refugee Commission (Michelle Brane' and dedicated Staff Members); and to the many other unrecognized individuals, non-profits, religious; to United Church of Christ, Kayla Bonewell, Pastor Church of the Open Arms, OKC, OK, for her advocacy of human rights and inclusion of all; and to activists individuals (Nathaniel Batchelor, T.J. McKinsey, the loyal weekly protestors at the I.C.E. office, OKC), secular organizations and churches; and *with deep appreciation for everyone who has helped or prayed for our Migrants ,who are each dearly loved.* Holding in our hearts all those who are migrating.

4

PREFACE

"Our immigration detention system locks up hundreds of thousands of immigrants unnecessarily every year, exposing detainees to brutal and inhumane conditions of confinement at massive costs to American taxpayers. Recently, mothers and children, who are mainly asylum seekers fleeing violence in Central America, have been detained in family detention centers.

The "lock 'em up" approach to detention is contrary to common sense and our fundamental values. In America, liberty should be the norm for everyone—and detention the last resort."

ACLU: https://www.aclu.org/issues/immigrants-rights/immigrants-rights-and-detention

ACKNOWLEDGEMENTS

Many thanks to those people who assisted with the publication of DESPERATE TRAVELERS. For his inspiration and mastery of the computer process of formatting and interfacing with the publishers and printers, a special thank-you to published author, Bill Boudreau.

I am grateful to those who have given their interest in the book and encouragement through the time of its growth and development: To members of Individual Artists of Oklahoma (IAO) Poetry Groups. Special appreciation and gratitude to professional educator Marci Brueggen my Editor; to Reviewers Katy Lantagne, Jessica Lantagne; to Pamela Vestal for her artistic assistance with the Cover Photo; and to fellow Authors: J.R. (Tex) Blair, Jennifer Long, Dorothy Alexander, Terri Cummings, and Larry Fishburn for the gems of inspirations contained within their own works.

Contents

Migrant Industrial Complex ~ a Tale of Desperate Travelers ~

Margaret Fletcher Malone

CHAPTER ONE-BUCKY

January

Abuela was on her knees. "Mom! There's a lady coming down the aisle, on her *knees*!" Fourteen-year-old Bucky leaned over the back of the pew, his blue eyes staring. Soon all the other congregants turned to stare at the very old Hispanic woman. Wrapped with a longish black Spanish-lace veil over her head and shoulders, her black dress was tucked up around her waist. Everyone, even the priest at the altar, couldn't help but stare at her.

Her head was tilted up, her hands clasping rosary beads against her breasts, her lips were mumbling. Black eyes, frozen into an intense gaze, were slightly tearing, glistening like beautiful large glass marbles. Her stare was focused on the life-sized figure of the crucified Lord hanging from a wooden cross high up on the wall behind the altar. She was seeing only Him. Talking to Him. Approaching Him slowly as if ready to hear aloud His *invitation* to continue coming to receive Him, the Love of her Life, in the bread of communion.

The first two pews of seated parishioners distinguished white middle-class residents of this rural southwest town, were stunned. Their church was not about *this* type of religion.

Comfortably seated in his usual aisle seat on the first row, Woodrow Smith felt deeply embarrassed at seeing this sight. It repulsed him. Her appearance and very presence offended his sensibilities of properness. She was a foreigner looking so old and wrinkled, choosing to hovel on her raw knees on the dirty floor, openly crying and spilling out her emotions of sentimentality. In spite of his revulsions, he followed her gaze up to the figure on the crucifix. He looked into its eyes. Did he see a movement? Did he see it returning her look of longing and its mouth mumbling loving phrases back to her? He had never before considered the molded figure on the crucifix in such a personal way. He felt very uncomfortable then frightened. What if that figure really were alive and suffering? A shiver went down his spine.

Woodrow's wife Irene sitting next to him poked him with her elbow and whispered harshly, "Go tell the priest to have the altar boys escort her out of here!" Woodrow stood and rushed up to the priest who had stepped down to the communion rail from the altar. With his priestly white vestment-draped arms raised, the priest was carrying a consecrated wafer holding it above the chalice in front of him. The priest waited for Woodrow to kneel, open his mouth and hold out his tongue. So, awkwardly Woodrow kneeled down and did so. The priest placed the wafer on Woodrow's tongue and passed on to the other congregants as they began filling up the kneeler as usual.

Finally, the last one waiting to be served the Bread of Life was her.

Woodrow's wife and the others were motioning and mouthing to the priest: "No! The *Mesicans* have their own church across the creek. Don't give it to her! You'll get them started coming over here! No! Send her away!" Seeing his parishioners' hostility, the priest began scowling in frustration and confusion, hesitating to offer the woman the Bread of Life.

Seeing the priest's indecision, Woodrow's wife finally stood up. She said sternly in a loud voice, "You better not!" The priest looked at the frail figure still on her knees, eyes closed holding open her small mouth. Her tears were now flowing freely down her cheeks in joyful anticipation of receiving her Beloved. The congregation was emotionally deafening with their silent chanting, "Turn her away! Turn her away!"

Behind closed eyes she felt the abrupt brushing across her face of the priest's flowing vestment sleeve as he turned away from her. He quickly walked away up the steps to the rear of the altar. He busied himself with putting away the golden communion plate and wiping out the silver chalice. She opened her eyes. Her face and her heart turned to stone as she realized that *her Lord had rejected her.* She slowly rose, turned and hobbled down the aisle, tears flowing in shame and grief as she pushed open the heavy wooden doors and left the church.

Sniffling, Bucky pressed his shoulder against his Mom's asking, "Why didn't he give her communion?"

CHAPTER TWO-JUAN

March

"Stop! Stop him!" screamed the store owner. Sixteen-year-old Juan running by, tripped over Bucky who was sitting on the curb reading his new comic book. Juan and Bucky rolled over each other getting caught in each other's unzipped coats. The store owner old man Orville was strong. With one hand he latched onto the front of Juan's shirt and pulled him up shaking the devil out of him. Orville shoved his huge hand into each of Juan's pockets. Coming up empty, Orville shoved Juan rolling him down the sidewalk. Orville cussed, "Damn wetback!" and returned inside the store.

Bucky recognized Juan from school. He was one of the older boys. Juan and his friends would stand around together on the grass outside of school joking in Spanish and laughing at their own comments. Bucky liked listening to them and would stand close by. They mostly ignored him but they were never mean to him. It wasn't that big of a school and most of the kids knew each other, even their names, although the older ones called all of the younger ones, "Kid," mostly.

Walking a shortcut through the park on his way home, Bucky was abruptly jerked off the path into the weeds and pushed to the ground. He started yelling. Juan smashed his hand over Bucky's mouth saying, "Just shut up!" So, Bucky did. Juan ordered Bucky, "Give it to me!" Shocked, Bucky asked, "What?" Juan pointed to his righthand coat pocket. Bucky reached in and pulled out a small glass container. It was a religious candle with a painted picture of Our Lady of Guadalupe dressed in blue. Juan grabbed it and looked at the picture for a long time. Watching him Bucky finally asked, "What's it for?"

Juan said tenderly, "My Abuelita (Grandmother)."

Juan began to sniffle. Bucky asked, "What's wrong?"

"She wants to die. She won't eat anymore. She sits on the back porch, so sad that she can't even cry."

"Why?"

"She said that Our Lord doesn't love her and that she can't bear His rejection of her. And that she doesn't deserve to live."

"Why?'

"She was late for Mass at our church about a month ago. She had to help my Mom with a neighbor's baby who was coughing and choking. So, by the time she arrived at church Mass was over. She wanted to go to Mass so bad, that she crossed the creek and went to the white church's later Mass. But she said that the Lord rejected her by not coming to her in communion and He is mad at her. And she just can't bear for Him to be mad at her because He is her life."

Bucky felt his eyes begin to sting. "I was there and saw her. It was awful. The first two pews of people didn't want the priest to give her communion and told the priest to turn her away, so, he did. And she had crawled all the way down the aisle on her knees!"

Juan looked shocked. "So that's why she thinks that God doesn't like her anymore?"

Bucky exploded, "It wasn't God! It was the priest and the people in the first two pews!"

Juan gritted his teeth. "Those damn *gringos*! I hate them! I'll kill them!" He began beating the ground with his fists. Then he noticed the candle. Bucky looked at him questioning.

Juan continued, "I was trying to figure out how to help my *Abuelita* to get God to like her again. I thought that maybe she could ask His mother to change her Son's mind. So, I stole this candle to give to her to light it to pray with."

Bucky looked at him, seeing his love for his grandma and how he didn't want her to die.

Juan picked up the candle and ran down the path. Standing up and brushing the grass off his jeans, Bucky walked home hoping that Juan's candle would help his *Abuelita* feel better.

As the days passed Bucky watched as Juan and his friends began to grow thin moustaches and sideburns. They began smoking cigarettes. One of them wore a black leather looking jacket. They all acted like they were cool. They began to spit in between their sentences. They liked looking at the girls but wouldn't talk to any of them.

During the next several days Bucky noticed that they huddled together talking secretly and kicking rocks. One afternoon as their group broke up to go home, Juan walked close by Bucky and whispered, "Hey, Buck, meet me at the white's church when it gets dark."

Bucky felt surprised and delighted. Juan had noticed him and called him Buck, not Kid, or Bucky. Of course, he would be at the church tonight.

CHAPTER THREE-LIGHTING ABUELA'S CANDLE

March

Buck showed up while it was still twilight. Venus the evening star was shining like a spotlight in the darkening sky just above the western horizon. Bulking-up in the northwestern sky the tall black storm clouds were flexing their bulging muscles blanching out flashes of heat lighting. Buck sat on the top step of the white's church waiting, looking up and down the street. About an hour later it had grown good and dark. He sensed movement in the shadows of the bushes beside the steps. Buck called out, "Juan?"

"Shhh! Come here."

"Where are you?"

"Over here."

Buck counted three others in the shadows. Juan pulled Bucky by his arm, found his foot, and placed it into the locked hands of the other boys. They lifted him up to the small window of the men's bathroom.

"Shove it open! It's unlocked. Crawl through and go open the side door for us. Be quiet!"

Buck felt excited but guessed he was doing something that he shouldn't be doing.

"Juan, is this okay? To get in this way?"

"Yes. Hurry up!"

Buck sucked in his stomach. Wiggling like a snake he finally popped through the shallow window, upside down. Bracing his falling body on his arms he fell on the marble terrazzo floor. Knowing this bathroom well he felt his way to the door and opened it. He couldn't see a thing in the narthex. He knew where the light switch was. Walking right to it he switched it on. He heard Juan and the other boys loudly whispering, "Turn it off! Turn it off!" So, he turned it off. Blackness. There was no way that he was going to step into the dark of the huge church and get lost wandering around. Feeling along the wall inside the large church sanctuary filled with pews, he found the light

15

switch next to the corner of the doorway and switched it on. Light flooded everywhere. He quickly ran to the side door and pushed the bar-handle. It clanked open. The boys rushed in and the door slammed behind them.

Juan told everyone to "Shut up!" He found a light switch next to the side door and switched it off. Darkness. No one moved. "Juan, are you still there?" No answer. No answer. Diego panicked, yelling, "I'm getting out of here!" The boys bumped into each other completely lost in the deep darkness. Juan finally said in a loud voice, "What the hell!" He switched on the light again.

The boys followed Juan who was walking through the aisles looking at the smooth shiny thick wooden pews. Making his way to the center aisle he asked Buck, "Now which pews were they sitting in telling the priest not to give communion to my *Abuelita*?"

Buck led them to the two front ones while stroking the carved wooden curls of the high seat-backs. "Right here. Woodrow and his wife Irene. Mr. and Mrs. Tully, who own the furniture store.

"Mr. Mitchell, the strawberry farmer. His wife and grown kids, all of them. They all were shaking their heads and saying 'No!' to the priest."

Juan, imagining them saying "No! No!" to his *Abuela*, became madder and madder. He began kicking their pews. He turned around looking for something with which to hit them. Spotting a fire-ax attached to the wall under a fire extinguisher he pulled it loose by its handle. Lifting the sharp blade high he crashed it down into those two pews. Splinters flew everywhere. Over and over, he swung it. His raging cussing eventually turned into sorrowful crying. His body gradually melted down onto the floor. He handed the hot blade to the other boys who took turns with it. The two pews were soon mauled to pieces. Seeing the destruction, Juan began to shout with bitterness, "I hate you! I hate you *gringos*! You killed my *Abuelita*!" Sinking to the floor and hugging his knees, he wailed loudly.

Buck slowly approached. He sat quietly beside him, put his skinny arm around Juan's shoulder and waited. When Juan's crying died down, Buck said sadly, "I didn't know she died. What happened? Didn't you give her the Our Lady of Guadalupe candle?"

Slumped over, Juan related in a flat voice, "She was already weak from starving herself. When I tried to hand the candle to her, she didn't have the strength to take it in her hands. So, I set it on her dresser where she could see it.

"Later, she could only lay in bed. I asked her if she wanted me to light the candle so that she could pray with it. She said, 'No I cannot pray. My soul has no more prayers. When my Lord wouldn't come to me, my heart began dying.'

" All she could do was look at that un-lit candle. She died during the night."

Juan rolled onto his back on the carpeted steps in front of the altar and stared at the vaulted ceiling. He looked up and around at all the saints in the walls' tall stained-glass windows surrounding him. All were staring down at him returning his gaze. One was smiling, holding a lily out to him. Another, was cuddling a lamb in his arms. Another, a lit candle. One window portrayed a rolling hillside covered with lots of people: men, women, and children. Jesus was carrying a basket full of bread on his arm. He was smiling, handing it out to all the people.
Juan studied it a long time. Finally, he whispered angrily, "This is all b***s**t! He stood up and yelled, "They're all *white. They* can have a *lit* candle! They can have *all* the bread that they want, with Jesus *smiling* at them! Even Jesus is *white!*

"This white's church is *lying* about what color Jesus is and has locked Him inside its for-whites-only building! I bet He hates being in here like I do. They wouldn't let my *Abuelita* come inside here to Him and get some of His bread! And she died without it. And now they have Him in here, stuck for thousands of years, painted white, in a stained-glass picture window!"

By now, Juan was really ranting. The boys were growing

scared of him and excited too.

Looking around, he blurted, "Let's get Him out of this whites-only jail! He wants to go outside to all the people. To *our* neighborhood across the creek. He wanted to come to *our* house to be with my *Abuela*. Where is He now? Where have they locked Him up? Over there, they have stored the extra bread wafers left over from communion! Come on. Diego, bring the ax!"

An ornate round domed cabinet crafted in silver was tucked away on a small altar built into the back wall of the sanctuary. The locked tabernacle was dimly lit by a small flickering candle in a red glass candle holder.

Juan tried to lift the tabernacle. No luck. Bolts fastened it to the surface of the stone altar. The tabernacle was attached on the backside and closed with an electric lock. An electric cord wired it directly into the wall.

Juan couldn't bear seeing all the ways that Jesus was trapped. He stepped back, lifted the ax, and yelled, "Get ready, Jesus, we're busting You out!" He slammed the ax blade down on the rounded top of the metal dome. The ax ricocheted out of Juan's hands straight up into the air, spinning end-over-end. Falling down blade first, it sliced between the tabernacle and the wall. The severed electrical wire sparked. Next, miraculously, the tabernacle's curved door slid sideways back into its track, slowly opening. It revealed its precious communion Resident. Juan held up the dim red candle which flickered on the boys' faces as they leaned forward to look inside. Bathed in soft candle light was the basket of white translucent bread wafers.

Juan reverently reached in and lifted out the basket. With both hands he carried it up the center aisle towards the exit. He motioned his head to Diego to push open the outside heavy wooden doors. Diego propped them open down-turning their rubber-toed small metal feet. Accompanied outdoors by his *amigos,* Juan carefully set down the basket on the edge of the top step. They gazed at a flight of twenty wide flagstone steps that cascaded downward to the sidewalk, the street, and outward to the town below.

Sweating and depleted by his anger and sorrow, Juan sank to his knees before the basket of wafers. He recalled Abuela's last conversation with him as she lay dying in her bed. With difficulty, she had told him,

"I can't bring up a prayer anymore or even talk to my Lord. My heart turned to stone when my Lord turned me away. Dying, I can only watch your candle, unlit. My faith that the Lord dearly loves me is gone. All hope of tasting Him is gone. As He wishes, so be it."

Juan, squatting on the steps talked to the wafers, saying, "Oh, my *Abuelita* and God. Now *I* will speak the prayers of your heart by lighting a candle for you. *I* will have the hope that you could not have for yourself that you were dearly loved by your Lord. The townspeople will see your lit candle and they'll be ashamed at how they treated you!"

Juan's face became determined and hard with anger and bitterness. Looking into his *amigos'* eyes, grabbing their hands, forming a circle, he gave the battle cry. "Let's do it! This is for you, *Abuelita*! "Watch this, *Abuelita. This will be your candle burning!* See, God really loves you! And I do too!"

Juan sprang up. He rushed back into the church down the side aisle to the wrought-iron rack of lit votive candles in their little red glasses. The rack was easily pushed on its squeaking little wheels. Following Juan the boys maneuvered it across the front of the nave to the center aisle. As they pushed it along the aisle towards the front doors, Juan took a lit candle from its red glass. He held it up high then hurled it like a fire-bomb into the pile of splintered wooden pews. The melted wax splattered as the flaming wick ignited the hated pews. Pausing momentarily to watch the leaping flames, the boys softly said to Juan, "Duende!" Juan wiped his splattered forearm free of the scalding drops of wax. Left behind were jagged scars that would forever remind him of this moment of vindication for his *Abuelita*.

One by one, Juan handed a flaming candle to each of the boys. They whooped and dodged flames grabbing and hurling lit candles everywhere. Scars from the spewing wax would leave physical memories of this moment for them as well. They continued to push the rack around the church emptying it of its lighted votive candles. Soon the rising leaping flames burned a hole through the top center of the vaulted ceiling creating a giant candle atop the church roof.

The town was lit up with the flames from the church as storm clouds moved in. Lightning flashes and ear-splitting thunder competed with the squeals of approaching sirens. Leaping down the steps away from the destruction and the approaching sirens the boys disappeared into the shadows of the night. Sheets of rain were beginning to engulf the town but were unable to quench the soaring flames consuming the church. Hell's fury had broken loose.

CHAPTER FOUR-IT'S NOT OVER

March

Buck noticed that his Dad had left the newspaper on the breakfast table. It was folded open to the article whose headline read "Burned Church Declared Total Loss." Buck caught his breath and had a moment of concern before he started reading the story. Who would be accused of causing it? What kind of trouble would they be in? He let out a sigh of relief as he started reading the article. It reported "The Fire Marshall's investigation concluded that the cause of the blaze was a bolt of lightning which he determined to be 'an act of god.' The church's pastor, Father Benito, stated that the Archbishop decided to not rebuild at this time."

The next day at school Buck asked around for Juan and his cousins, Diego, Gregorio and Armando. Juan's neighbor related that the four of them were no longer in town. He thought that they were probably headed back across the border to Mexico. After school Buck rode his bicycle across town to the home of Juan's family. Senora Elena Trujillo spoke kindly to him and wondered if Buck had any knowledge of where her son, Juan, and his cousins might be? Buck said No. She was worried that the border patrol might have picked them up and arrested them.

Her sister-in-law, Diego's mother, and Juan's *tia* (aunt), had been apprehended by I.C.E. (Immigration Customs and Enforcement) two years ago. The family heard that she and her youngest daughter, Maria, had been locked up in an I.C.E. family detention center in Dilly, Texas. The family had tried to contact her but were told that she had been transferred and they had been unable to locate her.

Senora Trujillo's eyes began to tear. "I'm so afraid that my Juan and Diego will disappear into I.C.E.'s prisons. My other sister, Carmen's, boys, Gregorio and Armando, are missing, too. Carmen died in Mexico during our escape from Honduras. So, I am taking care of all of the boys. I am very worried about them."

Buck did not want to worry her more by telling her about

21

their night at the church. While Senora Trujillo was talking, he remembered about the passing of Juan's *Abuela*. He offered his condolences to Senora Trujillo for the loss of her mother and left.

May

On the last day of school Buck's teacher asked each student to tell the class what he wanted to be when he grew up. "And, you, Bucky?" From looking out the window and wondering where Juan was, Buck stood up beside his desk and looked slowly at the teacher and scanned his classmates. He stated factually, "My Dad says that I will be a lawyer and work with him at the United Plant Company. My older brother William is graduating from college and is to work there too." The teacher waited. "And besides that, what do you want to be?"

Buck became quietly thoughtful. "Maybe a priest. But a *good* priest. Or maybe an agent in I.C.E. Border Patrol. Then I could ride a horse along the border in the mountains and look out for some friends who might be somewhere out there."

CHAPTER FIVE-THE JOURNEY

May

As if sensing that his young friend Buck was thinking about them, Juan, Diego, and their two cousins sat up from lolling in the sand under the shade of large grey-green mesquite bushes. They looked around admiring the open freedom of the desert, the mountains, and blue sky. Diego wondered aloud, "You know, if we get caught by I.C.E., they will put us in jail for burning down the church. They will send us to Dilly where my mother and little sister were locked up in the family detention center."

Juan felt the awakening of his lingering feelings of bitterness remembering how the *gringos* killed his *Abuelita*. He began to realize that if they were caught for starting the fire, they were going to be put into detention centers by the *gringos*. He felt how mean and unfair the *gringos* always treated his people. A hopeless thought entered his mind: "Now, it really doesn't matter what we do." He stood up, looked at his friends, and whispered loudly, "Diego, let's go get your mom and sister out of jail!" Bending low they quietly disappeared into the dense mesquite.

Juan, Diego, Gregorio, and Armando made a slow time of clawing their way through the dense foliage. They were getting hungry and thirsty and wanted to find a safe place where they could sleep. For a month! Finally, admitting it, they knew that they were lost. When it got dark, they slumped to the ground under the cover of bushes and slept in shifts. Each of them took a turn keeping watch for border patrol spotters. Ants, mosquitoes and scorpions gave them fits but the boys soon adapted to them as mere inconveniences, considering them the least of their worries.

From their sleeping place on a little hill one night, Diego pulling watch duty, was half dozing and half watching for shadows of movement in the surrounding landscape. He thought he smelled bacon cooking on a campfire. His stomach growled as he dozed in and out of sleep. If he were dreaming, he hoped

23

that he could dream up a huge platter of bacon, and *huevos,* with jalapenos, and hot tortillas, and.... His relaxed body finally fell backwards bumping his head on a rock. Awakened, he thought he was smelling bacon again. Crawling higher up the hillside, scanning to the east, he caught sight of a very small flicker of firelight in the distance. He surveyed the horizon in every direction. He saw nothing moving and felt a bit of relief. Hoping for a bit of good luck, he crept towards the flickering. Oh, *Dios,* it *was* bacon cooking! Among the brush he counted at least five figures with blankets around their shoulders sitting and laying around a miniscule campfire. Laying down, stretched low on his stomach, he waited quietly for about ten minutes, watching. They seemed to be ones like himself, hiding out. He wondered if he could risk approaching and asking for some bacon.

He felt a stalk of grass tickle his ear and brushed at it with his hand. Someone grabbed his hand, firmly holding it still, sitting on him with a knee pressing into his back. He couldn't move but he stayed quiet. He felt a breath near his ear and heard a woman's voice whisper *"Vamanos, amigo."* She released his hand and removed her knee from the middle of his back. Rolling over, he was too stunned to say a word. He silently followed her towards the campfire and the resting figures.

Sure enough, the group was just like him, hiding out. He learned that the woman's name was Josie. She fed him generously but not enough after days of having no food. He relished the freshly cooked bacon, two eggs, and two tortillas. He wanted to cry in gratitude for her kindness but she shushed him so the others could remain resting. After eating she offered him a blanket and he too stretched out to sleep, exhausted.

At first light he and Josie cautiously made their way back to Juan and the others. They all made their way back to Josie's camp. The amigos shared their cooked breakfast and quietly shifted themselves into position where they could remain for daytime safety and secrecy.

Josie shared that the group was waiting for their *coyote'* to return to finish leading them safely over the border. She was expecting that he would bring a truck that would transport them into Laredo, Texas. There, they were told, they could split up and easily travel to wherever they wished within the United States and start a new life. Of course, that story line was too good to be true.

Josie said that they were about ninety miles from the border inside Mexico just south of Laredo and east of Monterrey near the Sierra Picachos mountains in Nuevo Leon. They already had each paid the *coyote'* between $4,000 and $5,000. U.S. dollars. The *coyote'* had left them some food and said he would return soon. The *coyote'* worked for a cartel and he promised that the cartel's experience guaranteed them a safe border crossing because the cartel had a network of bribery involving certain U.S. border patrol agents and I.C.E. higher-ups *"No problemo!"*

As the sun rose higher, the leaves on the mesquite trees squeezed shut to conserve water leaving little shade for the thirsty travelers. The challenge was keeping out of sight of possible roving patrol spotters or their drones. In a day spent in anxious silence, they not only suffered from the heat and but worried about what might happen to them as they waited for word from their *coyote'*.

That evening, around the tiny campfire of small twigs they shared their stories. An exhausted and silent *Abuela* Carolina squatting back on her heels quietly sipped from the cup of *yerbe' mate'* passed among the travelers. She was holding and rocking a small child belonging to one of the other women.

THE MIGRANT

> *The journey had been*
> *So rough, long, life-threatening,*
> *She could not recall:*
> *Places, she laid her head,*
> *Things, once held,*
> *Lessons, once learned,*
> *Bravery, with which she led.*

25

*The **now** was all that felt much real:*
Soft crackling comfort of campfire,
Resting, squatting quietly on her heels,
Someone's child, sleeping lovely in her arms,
The kindness of the passing cup,
Of sweetened yerba tea.

Oh my, oh my,
Her life was stripped,
As worn away, as
Many soles of countless shoes.

*Leaving only **herself**,*
A piece of sacred art:
"Living gratitude."

Three of the immigrants had left Honduras because cartel gangs were threatening to rape them or to force them into recruitment to serve in their militias. They feared being kidnapped for ransoms or killed just because the gangs could get away with it. Or anything to make a buck off the fleeing and helpless souls.

MIGUEL'S HISTORY LECTURE

Miguel shared that he had been a college history teacher in Mexico City but had returned to Nicaragua to help his family escape. Sadly, he returned too late to help them. They had all been killed by a local gang. Now, he was wandering the countryside taking time in an effort to walk off his grief. His grandparents and other relatives had once owned farms as did other villagers. They had raised their own food in the fertile valleys where there were always a surplus of crops to share and sell. There were no gangs then as everyone was living sustainably, helping each other.

In his college teacher lecture tone, he continued. "But then our government was forced to sign over all of the most fertile lands to the U.S. corporations, such as, the United Plant Company. My family members and their neighbors were forced to work almost as slave labor for the U.S. corporate farms. They lost their family homes and farms and began living in poverty.

"That's when the gangs started forming an alternative black-market economy and forcing us to work for them in the illegal drug industry by growing, harvesting, packaging, and transporting as 'human mules.' Women were forced into prostitution within a network that promoted trafficking of women and children in the sex trade. Men, women, and children were forced into the cartels' private militias which were involved in kidnappings for ransom and other kinds of extortions for money.

"The U.S. government removed our democratically selected president and leaders. The U.S. replaced them with puppet dictators and militia who were trained in American academic institutions founded for just those purposes. Upon being returned to their home countries and installed as presidents 'recognized' by the U.S., they were then supplied arms and U.S. military advisors.

"The puppet governments are controlled by the U.S. government's organizations such as the CIA, IMF (International Monetary Fund), and U.S. private banks and business corporations. The drug cartels were formed and permitted to operate in order to keep the people from protesting and unable to organize and become self-governing. The cartels are high-paying customers of the U.S. weaponry manufacturers.

"The foreign aid delivered to these countries is paid directly to members of the U.S. military industrial complex of weapons' manufacturers located in the U.S. Their weapons products are then given as in-kind foreign aid to the puppet dictators. Our impoverished citizens never receive a dime of the so-called foreign aid to be able to meet their basic needs of food, clothing, and shelter.

"Thus, the common people live in abject poverty with no

means to support a local economy to work their way out of their poor living conditions. Sociologically, this is identified as a type of covert or neo-colonialism and government oppression.

"Soon, the cartels infiltrated the government as well as the national oil company. The cartels siphon off oil from the pipelines to sell for their own profit. They now largely control the transportation network of seaports, railroads, and the trucking companies. It is estimated that about forty percent of the U.S. Border Patrol officials are corrupted by the cartels' smuggling businesses.

"Opportunistically, cartels have cashed in on the business of hiring out *coyotes* for immigration services. Ironically, the cartels have created the need for *coyotes*. One cartel's *coyote* is needed to protect immigrants from predations by other cartels. To avoid the attacks of preying cartels and the need to pay the exorbitant prices of *coyotes*, migrants attempt to gather in caravans to travel from their home countries to the U.S. seeking the safety of numbers.

"Just follow the money to see who is *receiving and profiting* from the border and immigration control expenses paid by the taxes of the common U.S. citizens. While not widely publicized, the information is documented and when known makes it easier to understand the problems of illegal immigration.

"The U.S. government, which is controlled by the big corporations, want their oil companies and United Plant Company-type big corporations to continue to control and profit from their farms and businesses located in our Central American countries of Honduras, El Salvador, Nicaragua, and Guatemala. The U.S. has created the monster of the "Illegal Immigration Industrial Complex." This growing group of immigration related businesses is opportunistically growing fat and rich from the sufferings of thousands of innocent people.

"The Illegal Immigration Industrial Complex, those companies and organizations profiting in the U.S, are deciding that it is "smart business" and desirable to create the trade-off of forcing suffering and impoverished people to flee for their lives away from their home countries. The cartels are encouraged to keep the poor terrorized and local governments de-stabilized to prevent any effective protests against the U.S. exploitation of their countries' natural resources. The church leaders sell out, too, and won't denounce the criminals for fear of retaliation.

"In fact, the U.S. government's repressive immigration laws were enacted to benefit this Illegal Immigration Industrial Complex! Those business owners avail themselves to take advantage of the cheap labor of our desperate and poorest people who are seeking to save their very lives through migrating and seeking asylum.

"Those U.S. corporate predators are becoming wealthy through the U.S. government's use of private contracts. These include private contracts to build border walls, staff border patrols, build and staff private detention centers, sell arms and munitions to puppet dictators and to drug cartel militias, and more. They are contracted to expand private immigration services of attorneys, judges, parole officers, and growing other private contracts for related migrant businesses."

"Somewhat unacknowledged, one rapidly growing element profiting from illegal immigration are the mobs. Much of the wealth, globally, and increasingly in the U.S., is controlled by various mobs. The Russian mob of oligarchs, especially violent and ruthless, has infiltrated the U.S. government and through favors, loans, extortion, and blackmail controls many politicians. Foreign entities are also influencing elections.

"It is now publicly and globally acceptable for governments to be controlled by mobs and dictators. *The role of citizens is now to be the disenfranchised impoverished workers for the wealthy one-percent of the population.*

"The bottom line for us immigrants and asylum seekers, is to not be fooled into thinking that we are the problem. Rather, we are the *victims* who are being used by the wealthy oligarchs to **destabilize** every country's society. When citizens turn on each other, like when the whites hate us brown people, everyone becomes afraid of each other. Everyone then votes for strong dictators to take over and establish law and order, hoping to have safety from 'those others.'

"That model of 'destabilizing societies' is now in progress in the U.S. We migrants, us! sitting around this campfire, are being forced to play the role of de-stabilizers (as invading hordes) while *each one of us is simply trying to stay alive.* The wealthy oligarchs are causing this situation: the mobs, the cartels, the corporate billionaires, and the corrupt politicians in every country. The citizen voters who support it have been brainwashed through fear to continue voting for the 'strongman' who, of course, increases oppression. He removes the democratic freedoms of citizens and declares martial law and national emergencies to continue his dictatorial rule. This makes for a self-reinforcing cycle of oppression of citizens."

Everyone passively nodded their heads 'yes' and murmured "*Claro.*" Miguel's animated speech seemed to solidify their feelings of closeness to each other. They rested in their weariness.

Josie asked the lookout, "Do you see the truck coming yet?" Privately, Miguel covered his eyes with his brown hands thinking to himself, 'Of course not! No one is coming to help us. It's up to us to get across the border on our own. Lies, lies, lies!'

He said aloud, "If they don't come by tomorrow, let's make some other plans. *Si, amigos?*"

CHAPTER SIX-WASHINGTON, D.C.

June

At the end of the school year, Buck was in Washington, D.C. He was a member of a student group from his high school on tour of the National Capital. His white sneakers with their flaming red tongues standing up, carried him up and down the steps of monuments, museums, and government stone buildings that looked like fortresses. His blue eyes were dry from looking upwards at the massive structures. Used to the sights of open pastures and far off mountains of his desert Southwest, the many surrounding stone walls felt oppressive. Under his loose bleached-blond hair, Buck's brain was saturated with images of a bustling city.

The tour guide announced that they were taking a break. Everyone was on his own until they were to meet back here in two hours. Sitting on the top step at Lincoln's oversized stone feet, Buck gazed with him out over the city where politicians were struggling for power and money. His eyes rested on a small flock of pigeons pecking and gurgling nearby. His mind vegged-out watching their bobbing heads of iridescent purples and greens. Ignoring him, they were absorbed among themselves in maneuvering and positioning for dominance over whomever was closest. Buck looked up at Lincoln's sad face and said, "So, Mr. President, you're watching the Washington pigeons, too?"

Following Lincoln's stone-eyed gaze Buck was able to pick out the various government buildings that they had visited. He found the I.C.E. headquarters with its stockade façade. Buck's trip to Washington was an important event both for himself and the family. His father had arranged with their local congressman's office for his brother William to have a personal tour of I.C.E. agency national headquarters. The tour was to include for William an employment interview with one of the assistants to a deputy director. His father's employer, United Plant Company, had working relationships with many I.C.E. personnel so his father had obtained several high-level references for William.

Buck's father had outlined the plan that William was to begin employment with I.C.E since he had just graduated from a University with a partial online Criminal Justice degree, as a recommended affiliation with DHS (Department of Homeland Security). At the same time, this summer Buck would intern, also, within the DHS. The two sons would room together during William's basic training. Their father emphasized that they should be alert to making networking relationships within I.C.E.

Their first assigned location was to be in Glycol, Georgia where William would be enrolled in the Customs and Border Patrol Officer training program. Following that, he would be assigned to Artesia, New Mexico for advanced training. After working as an Agent for several years, William was to sign on with United Plant Company for a long career.

His Dad speculated that the Company might even send William to law school to work in their legal department. Buck was to accompany William for "the experience of networking"
As pre-planned, William met Buck near the entrance of the I.C.E. headquarters. As they approached the formidable I.C.E. building, Buck envisioned seeing burley white men dressed in khaki uniforms carrying side-arm holsters and pistols. He wondered if William would be required to dress likewise. What would it feel like to carry a gun? Would William be expected to actually shoot it? And who would he be shooting? Would it be Juan's mother and little sister? The familiar memory of Juan rose in his mind. Again, he wondered where Juan was and what were he and his cousins doing now. He hoped that our Lady of Guadalupe was watching over them.

William and Buck identified themselves and checked in with the I.C.E. receptionist, a pretty and serious young woman with bright brown eyes, black wire-rimmed eye-glasses, and light brown hair, pulled back into a bun. She was sitting on a high stool behind a thick, bullet-proof glass enclosure. William talked to her through the chest-high, small horizontal slits in the glass. Under the pane, through a chrome-scooped hole, she slipped badges to them with their names and photos on them. Buck wondered how did they take this photo of him standing here, just now? He looked up and around at the ceiling. She buzzed open a door. A security guard escorted them through multiple halls and floors. They ended up in a waiting room. They joined the other men in chairs, sitting quietly, lining the walls. Some of them had open briefcases on their laps and were shuffling papers. Seeing the various serious-faced "suits" sitting around him he recalled in a flashback memory that night at the church with Juan.

FLASHBACK

That night, after the boys had placed the Bread outside on the top step to overlook the town, they had walked down the long flight of stairs. Juan led them as they wandered through the back streets of the town. In the darkness, Juan whispered to Buck to follow him through an alley to the back door of the local tavern. Juan knocked three times, loudly and fast, then three times, softly and slowly.

A cook cracked open the door, recognized Juan, and let in the boys. Juan whispered, *"Ola, Santiago. Por va for, comina, Primo?"* Santiago led them into the kitchen and pointed to a table used by the kitchen staff. Santiago silently placed his finger over his lips. He hurried away to the grill where he sprinkled a large handful of fajita meat slices, chopped pieces of red tomatoes, white onions, and green peppers which fell onto the hot grill in a sizzling heap. The boys became engrossed with the rising steam and delicious hot smells.

Their table was pushed against a thin white plastic folding screen wall. It separated the kitchen area from a row of customer booths on the other side, inside the main room of the tavern. The boys realized that they were listening to conversations of customers who had no idea that they could be heard. In the booth closest to them, the customers, all men, were clinking beer mugs together, joking, and crudely dissing each other. Buck suddenly recognized their voices.

The gravelly voice was Mr. Bates, the Manager of the United Plant Company where Buck's father worked. The wheezy voice was Mr. Hartz, the newspaper editor. The deep voice was Mr. Grey, the local I.C.E. Director. The high-pitched voice was Mr. Jake Crawford, the local congressman. The clipped voice was Mr. Dale, the sheriff. Buck did not "get" their jokes that made them laugh. He was able to follow most of their conversation that now reached a lull.

Mr. Bates' voice became guarded and serious. He had turned the topic to "wetbacks" who were "taking advantage" of America by living here. Newspaper editor, Mr. Hartz, chimed in that, "Because they entered America illegally they deserve to be treated like cheap-labor, even like slaves. They don't deserve employment benefits, safety conditions, health care, insurance, minimum wages, social security benefits, drivers' licenses, voter registration, passports or I.D.s and their kids don't deserve getting our good education or protection by our police and fire departments." I.C.E. Director Grey said, firmly, "Well, our working policy is to treat them as criminals who are probably dangerous. They should all be behind bars." Sheriff Dale, said, "Damn straight!" He addressed the congressman directly.

"Jake, we send you to Washington to make sure the laws are made to take care of us, the real citizens, and not those dirty illegals. And we local law enforcement professionals want laws that give us the authority to arrest them and immediately decide who and when to deport. We can tell by the color of their skin and their jabbering who they are. We don't want Washington telling us who we can and can't arrest and kick-out of our own country!"

United Plant Company, Manager Bates' voice took on a calm, reassuring tone. "Now, gentlemen. Let's, also, look at the business side of these people. It's good for us citizens economically to not make it possible for these illegal immigrants to become legal, you know? They don't have access to benefits and protections as long as we can keep them in an illegal status.

"We business owners can pay them below minimum wages, with no health insurance, expensive safety protections, or retirement pensions. And the federal government's social security administration loves it when the illegals have to use fake social security numbers because, as illegals, they still have to pay social security taxes. About 14%, deducted from their paychecks. But they'll never get to collect any of it when they reach retirement age because, officially, they do not exist in the social security system. They're not eligible for Medicare either. Now, is that smart business on our part, or what?" He laughed.

"In fact, we company managers can keep them in line pretty easy by threatening to call I.C.E. and have them deported. We like seeing them squirm and jump up and do whatever we tell them to do! They can't sue us! And they can't vote!" He laughed, again. He then addressed the congressman:

"So, Jake, you just make sure that Congress slows way down on ever doing anything about immigration law reform, you hear? We have those dirty wetbacks just where we want them!" He and the others murmured "yes" all around.

I.C.E. Director Grey added, "Yeah, Jake. Just appropriate more and more money for us at I.C.E. and local law enforcement agencies. Right, Sheriff? To hire more deputies, buy more weapons, build more detention centers and jails, and build higher walls. It's good business for us. We'll keep control of these illegal dogs, won't we, Sheriff?" Everyone laughed.

After the laughing died out, Congressman Jake Crawford spoke. "Okay, boys. I hear you. And I'm your man to work with our friends back in Washington, D.C. But we need your help, too, you know. Bates, I need you to shake the money tree over at United Plant Company for contributions from their PAC (Political Action Committee). My re-election's coming up next year. And, the way things work in Congress, the Speaker of the House won't even listen to any proposals for regulations or legislation until he receives a minimum contribution of five thousand dollars to his personal "non-profit" corporation. And to get a committee chairman and members to read the proposal,

35

much less put it on their docket. Yep! They all have to have their 'donation needs,' too. It's not cheap up there. But we can produce the best legislation for you that money can buy." He chuckled.

"And, the good news is that we Republicans are now the majority and in control thanks to good patriotic people like you. We got all three branches of the federal government and most of the state branches, too. So, we are all on the same page on the 'business value' of the immigrant issue. One word of caution for the future: Just watch out locally that no Democrats start getting elected to town councils, school boards, county jobs, or state legislatures. Those people can start the crack-in-the-dam, if you know what I mean. Keep a sharp eye on who is allowed to vote, especially. Okay?"

Newspaper Editor Hartz, not to be left out, put in a good word for himself. "My editorials frequently alert the townspeople as to how the migrants are cheating the rest of us out of our hard-earned tax dollars and public services. And my reporters are damn bloodhounds for any negative stories about illegal apprehensions. I don't mind bragging a bit that some of our stories scare the hell out of people. Especially when the illegal suspects 'remain at large.' He snorted. "And it sells my papers, too. And, before you have to ask, Jake. Yes, I'll write an editorial endorsing you. And I'll run another complimentary political ad for your re-election. You can count on me."

Congressman Jake closed the evening with handshakes and jokes. Buck could hear the men's shoes scraping out of the booth and walking away.

Buck, Juan and the boys finished eating their delicious, and free, supper in stunned silence. They slipped out of the back door of the tavern shocked at what they had heard. Hands in pockets, heads slumped, the innocence of their belief in the American Dream trailed behind them like flipped-away cigarette butts and hocked-up spit in the gutters. They stayed in the shadows of the alleys on their way back to the church.

BACK TO I.C.E. HEADQUARTERS

Buck had kept the experience of that night of the burning of the church a secret. He had wondered how those men talking in the cafe could be so mean. Feeling a personal regret, he sometimes wished that he and Juan and the other boys hadn't actually destroyed the church that belonged to everyone, not just to them. Maybe, he could talk about it with William later.

Back in the waiting room, reverie over, Buck studied the faces of the "suits" sitting in silence and wondered what deals they would be making with the I.C.E. bosses. He wondered what William, as a border patrol agent and then himself as an intern, were getting themselves into by joining Homeland Security's I.C.E.

William's interview was trouble-free: "Yes, I know your congressman, Jake Crawford. Jake plays golf with my boss occasionally. Yes, I was told that your father works as a manager at the United Plant Company." The assistant drew the short interview to a close: "Yes, you both have been approved to start immediately. You will be notified of the details within the week. Thank you for coming in. Good day." And they left.

Buck felt relieved to be outside in the sunlight and fresh air. He noticed that on the sidewalk corners, there were more small flocks of pigeons, gurgling and pushing among themselves. Buck looked up the hill to the stone statue of the stone seated Lincoln and gave him a tip of a salute of understanding of what this town was all about.

CHAPTER SEVEN-HUPT TWO THREE

June

Buck learned that upon becoming a new hire of I.C.E., William's mission was to become proficient in semi-military style areas of law enforcement.

William seemed to take the new situation in stride. The class room studies were manageable. He was able to accomplish the boot camp exercises of physical workouts and marching by putting his mind into a semi-numb state. Time passed in a rhythm of sun-up till sun-down and "hut-hut-hut" marching. Buck wondered what his own summer internship would entail. Soon, the OIC (Officer in Charge) with authority, let him know.

Buck showed up in the OIC's office, as instructed, on an early Monday morning. The seasoned officer and staff grinned when he walked in. Buck was dressed in his jeans and baseball cap with bright blue eyes and a hesitant smile on his boyish face. Buck flinched at their knowing smiles but stood up straight and announced that he would turn fifteen-years-old next month. On July 4th.

The OIC took a rough delight in ordering Buck to clean the bathrooms and jog, in the heat of the day, around the inside perimeter of the compound, surrounded with high, razor-blade-topped wiring. Buck enjoyed being active in the outdoors. He explored the various buildings on the compound, especially, the corrals and stables where the patrol horses were sheltered. He would take his breaks there. He liked hearing the soft, rhythmic clanking of the metal windmill blades harmonizing with the sloughing of the wind in the pine trees.

The Staff Sergeant assigned to the Horse Patrol Command noticed Buck's lingering presence in their area. It occurred to the Sergeant that, perhaps, he could request that Buck be assigned to his Command, "to learn Horse Patrol procedures." And, at the same time, to perform some of the less desirable duties, of course. So, it happened. Buck began cleaning out stalls, carrying sacks of grain and bales of hay, feeding the horses, hosing and scrubbing them down, and riding them to keep them exercised and ready for patrols. It wasn't long until Buck was informed that due to his "exemplary achievements," he was being given an advanced opportunity that could be considered a type of promotion. He was to conduct night patrols. On his own! Buck was delighted.

Riding horse patrol was his favorite part. He breathed in deeply the mountain air. During the day, it was hot with the smell of road dust and, at night, cool and pungent with the smell of skunk and pine. For the next month he rode on his pony under the stars on the high mountain ridges overlooking the river valley. He marveled at the millions of miles of stars, delighting in their glimmers on the ripples of the distant flowing river. He often wondered if Juan and his friends might be wandering somewhere like that. During the long nights, in companionship, he gave his mount the reins to graze freely. His pony could always find a mouthful of grass somewhere. However, for himself, Buck never found a migrant.

Bunking together, Buck and William enjoyed their brotherhood. During their talks from their army cots in their small barracks room, after lights-out, Buck asked William if he really wanted to work for I.C.E. William began to ramble, slowly falling asleep: "You know, what I really like to do is construction. I didn't talk about it with Dad, but I took as many courses as I could in construction at the University. If Dad would have pressed me about 'wasting your time,' I would have told him that I was required to have so many electives. But I actually enrolled in more than a few.

"And I really like the smell of freshly sawed lumber. You know, while here in Georgia, we really ought to visit some of their famous lumber mills, don't you think? Just imagine how good that would smell, a huge lumber mill filled with fresh-cut Georgia Southern Pine!" Soon, William began to exhale loud breaths which soon turned into full blown snores.

There was something about those nights of talking to each other in the dark. They couldn't see each other's faces. Buck wondered if his brother would have been ashamed of him if he told some awful things about himself. There was a feeling of privacy between them that felt safe, even safe enough to tell one's secrets, deepest secrets. And, to a brother, too. Several times Buck almost told William about that night when he was in on that episode of burning down the church.

Buck sometimes really wanted to tell someone about it. How he had been there. How he had not tried to stop the others, but, also, how he, himself, didn't actually throw any lit candles. Well, just that one. And, the stinging burn of the scalding wax that sprayed on his arm had almost made him cry. Buck reached up on his arm and rubbed the smooth scar. And, how he was secretly glad and hoped that Juan's *Abuela* was watching and that, seeing how they were getting back at the whites' church for *her,* made things better. At the last minute, before telling William, Buck always stopped himself, mainly, because his throat tightened up and started to ache.

All too soon, June was over. Buck would miss his pony. The OIC called him in and reported that Buck's father learned about the duties of his internship. His father requested that "to balance out his learning opportunities," he be reassigned to an I.C.E. legal office in Philadelphia. The OIC replied on the phone to Buck's dad, in his strong authoritarian tone that, "As his father, you can now take pride in your son's new sense of self confidence, something his internship work here at I.C.E. has helped your young man develop." Defensively adding, "And you should see how sharp he looks in his uniform and regulation haircut!" He lamely ended the conversation with "And his new black shoes are always highly polished, Sir."

So, William put his little brother on the Amtrak train for his trip up the East Coast with a wave and encouragement that "It will be a good experience for you." William told him that their father wanted him to "Make as many networking connections as you can. And, Dad sent this extra cash for emergencies." which

40

William pressed into his hand. With the $100 bill warming his pocket, Buck waved good-bye to his brother from behind the train window as it pulled out of the Georgia station, looking handsome in his uniform and his polished black shoes.

CHAPTER EIGHT-IN THE WILDERNESS

March

Miguel, ended his story of how he had ended up with the other migrants, hiding out in the Mexican desert. They were journeying to enter *The Promised Land of the U.S.,* trekking all the way from Honduras. He wanted to get as much rest as possible before proceeding with them on the next leg of the trip. He had given up on waiting for the cartel's *coyote'* to return to lead them across the border. He hoped that the others would agree with him to wait no longer. Miguel laid down on his blanket and tried to sleep in the heat of the day.

As most were dozing, the only sounds were of the occasional fly making abrupt moves, buzz-humming from someone's leg to his arm, and then over to someone's sweaty cheek. Rosie, wakeful, turned to Juan who was darting his eyes back and forth, searching the horizon for any movements, especially watchful for border patrol agents. Or, hopefully, the cartel's expected coyote'.

In a quiet voice, she asked, "You said that there were four of you. But I count only three. Where is the other one?" Juan jerked a glance at her. He said in a soft and sad voice, "I don't know what happened to him. One morning we woke up and he was gone. We followed his tracks until they were blown over with sand. They were headed towards a high plateau that seemed to have a haze around it. We called and called for Gregorio but could never locate him. So, we had to move on." Juan stopped speaking and grew tense, then lowered his head, covered his eyes with his hands and softly cried. "I would give anything to find him again."

Finally, Josie said, "That is not a good thing, him heading towards that plateau. Our custom is to not speak of that place for fear of bringing its curse upon our heads. It's not a good place for your Gregorio to go." Upset, Juan looked at her, not knowing what to say. Seeing Juan's distress, Josie said, "Okay, I will tell you about it, but first I will say a prayer to Our Lady of

Guadalupe for protection for all of us." She closed her eyes and made the sign of the cross on her forehead and chest.

"We call it *La Place de las Animas* or Ghost Mountain. At the base of it on all sides is a very deep arroyo with loose gravel walls that slip loose and slide down the deep sides of the canyon, carrying whoever is stepping on it and burying him alive, like quicksand. It is said that many animals and people are buried there because they did not know about its trap. Only rabbits seem to be able to cross it freely without danger to themselves. The reason that it is called "*las animas*" mountain is that some have reported seeing wandering on top of the plateau the ghosts of those who were buried alive. Their spirits remain trapped up there."

Juan stood up and looked in all directions again searching for his friend, Gregorio, hoping to see him come walking out of the desert. Juan finally spotted the mound of haze in the far distance that he knew was the plateau where Gregorio was headed. Juan wanted to run towards it and rescue his friend before he was trapped.

Josie could see what Juan was thinking and motioned for him to sit down. "There is something else. My *Abuela* told me that her *Abuela*, Maria, had told her that only certain people are drawn towards that Place or can even see it. It seems that Maria's family owned a donkey that was very stubborn, irritable, and even mean to every other animal or person that came near it. Her father tried and tried to soften the animal's disposition but it remained obstinate. It even kicked to pieces the cart that it was pulling. The cart was very important to the family's livelihood. One day while it was kicking at a near-by chicken pecking up grains of oats, the donkey, Jose', went into a fit, broke through the rail fence and ran off towards that *Place*.

"Maria's father sent her to bring back the donkey. She followed it all day coming very near to the *Place*. When evening came she made a small campfire and settled down on her blanket. As she was dozing, she noticed the fire began to crackle loudly. In the flames she saw the faces of many spirits, all talking to her asking for help to escape from the plateau.

"The stories they told were that, now, as ghosts, they mingled with the others who also had been drawn there. They put together their stories and realized that they all had a certain thing in common. Each one in his own way had destroyed something important that belonged to others. They all had their own reasons: some had been in a rage; some were wanting revenge to get back at another; the more adventuresome had wanted to experience the thrill of the action of destroying something. Others wanted to show that they were the most powerful and to have everyone be afraid of them while some just enjoyed seeing others suffer.

"In fact, each one was still feeling the same way. As they told their stories, they became violent all over again and began fighting and trying to destroy each other. Being in ghost form, they could not really destroy anyone or anything, so, they eventually got bored and were still. Occasionally, one or another would try again to act out but would be whacking only thin air.

"The faces reported that they were all trapped with an occasional new animal or person being drawn towards the *Place* to join them. They begged Maria to help free them. Maria was exhausted and eventually fell asleep as the campfire slowly burned down to smoky ashes. The next morning, following the donkey's tracks she was led to the edge of the arroyo. The hoof prints disappeared down into the steep gravel grave.

"Maria wiped away a tear about the sad fate of the family donkey, Jose'. She backed away from the edge of that dangerous canyon and made her way over to an outcrop of a rock cliff to rest in the shade before returning to her parents' home.

"The cliff was formed into a wind-blown smoothly sculpted indention shaped like a tall, rounded, scooped-out column stretching about thirty feet wide and forty feet tall. Surprised, Maria found it lovely and inviting. Wild desert rose bushes were blooming in the protected area. Approaching closer she found a small spring-fed pool softly bubbling with clear, cool water. She wondered if she were dreaming and rubbed her eyes and pinched the back of her hand. She sat next to the pool, taking it all in. Suddenly, within her mind, she clearly heard a woman's voice say to her, 'Maria?' She answered, '*Si*?' The voice continued, 'I am Our Lady of Guadalupe and I, too, have heard the crying out of the faces trapped on the plateau. Would you like to help me to free them?' Maria immediately answered aloud, '*SI*'.

"The voice resumed, 'Then, this is my plan for them. It, also, will be an example for others in similar circumstances, who still remain alive on earth, to follow, if they choose.' Maria was listening closely and feeling the warmth and caring of Our Lady that made her, too, feel loving and caring towards the trapped souls. Maria asked, 'What is your idea and what do you want me to do?'

"'The idea is to build a chapel here in this grotto followed by the building of many other churches that allow people to work together and to help each other. You see, these souls here are trapped by their sins. Each of their sins is the same. **There is only one sin**. You may wonder: What is such a sin?

"'A sin occurs when someone destroys the only thing that someone else can possess. **The only and most important thing that belongs to each person that can be destroyed by others is one's awareness and faith that each one of us is loved dearly**. Knowing that one is dearly loved results in a confidence and understanding that we are all connected to everything else with this love-thread.

"'The way out of the trap of their self-built hell is for these souls to engage in building and repairing what they destroyed: individuals' faith that each one is dearly loved.

"'So, here is what I want you to do. When the time is right and the right people appear, tell them what I have taught you. Tell them to build. Tell them to start by building a chapel here. Tell them to offer the opportunity to the trapped souls here to free themselves by learning that each person is dearly loved. Do you understand?' Maria felt excited and said, 'Yes!' And the voice became silent.

"Before Maria left that lovely spot, she picked up stones and laid them in a line end-to-end with a space in-between. Looking down at them along the row she said, 'That's where the door is going to be.'"

Josie pulled out her canteen and lifted it taking a long slow drink of water. Juan had followed every word of her account. He pictured Gregorio standing on the edge of the arroyo, looking down. He was silently yelling at Gregorio, "No! No! Wait right there! I'm coming!"

CHAPTER NINE-OVER THERE

Juan stood up. He brushed sand off the seat of his jeans. He looked around the campsite for a bottle of water. Josie asked him, "What are you doing?" "I'm going to keep Gregorio from falling into that arroyo. And I've got to hurry." Josie questioned, "How? What if he is being drawn there like the others? Then, what are you going to do?" Juan stood still thinking then said. "Why? What has he done to deserve that?" Josie replied, "I don't know. Has he ever destroyed peoples' stuff? Their feeling of being *loved dearly*?" Juan thought a while then muttered, guardedly, "Well, he might have helped burn down some white peoples' church one time." Shocked, Josie said, "Oh."

Finding another spot to where the shade had moved, Juan sat down, hiking-up his knees. He silently tried to figure things out. Josie watched him and tried to guess what had happened about the church burning down. She ventured the question, "Did you, too, have something to do with that? The church burning?" Juan squirmed. "Maybe, a little." "So, maybe you are being drawn to *la Place de las Animas* just like Gregorio?" Juan stiffened. "Hell, No! I don't want to die! What are you talking about?"

Josie casually stated, "Just saying. Think about it. Were there any people that the church belonged to that would feel unloved after you and Gregorio burned it? Destroyed it? What about them?" Juan was caught completely off guard. He had never considered making anyone feel that they were unloved, especially, those mean *gringos*. Then, angry thoughts flashed through his head, "Good! Now they know how it feels! They should suffer a lot, just like my *Abuelita* did when they caused her to feel that she wasn't loved by her Lord, when the priest denied her communion!"

All this was too much for Juan to handle. He stood up again and said in a rough tone, "I don't care about any of that! I'm going to get Gregorio before he falls into that arroyo! Does anyone want to come with me and help?"

Following Josie's advice and reasoning that they would be

traveling in the direction of the border anyway, the group of migrants packed up their gear. In single file and spaced about twenty yards apart, they followed Josie, Juan, Diego, and Armando. They were hiking north towards "a plateau covered in haze" that only the three boys could see.

The plateau's haze began to shimmer, appearing like wavering heat waves in a mirage. The ghosts there, *los amimas,* were alerted and disturbed into a swirling mass of faces within a heaving atmosphere of grey-blue clouds circling the mountain top. Watching the approaching party of hikers they wondered if, like themselves, the hikers were to be ensnared on their high-top place of entrapment.

The migrants hiked through the remainder of that day, through the night, and into the next day stopping for a brief rest as someone felt he could go no further. They finally arrived at an outcrop of a rock cliff with a pool of spring water where they collapsed, exhausted. Juan, Diego, and Armando took turns calling for Gregorio. Spreading out they searched for him where there might be shady spots or protected areas.

At last, they found him barely alive scrunched up into a small cave-like depression under a large boulder. They dragged him out and to their campsite by the pool of spring water. They soaked his dehydrated body in the pool cooling his body and quenching his thirst. On a campfire Josie cooked bacon, huevos, and tortillas coaxing him back to life with hot food and her motherly attention.

He remained collapsed on the ground while the sitting boys took turns holding his head on their laps stroking his face and hair. Trying to keep him awake they smiled, cried, and cooed over him like their long, lost puppy dog. Gregorio would look up at them, smile, and then sleep some more. Gradually, he revived.

Sitting around their campfire, Juan asked Gregorio, "So, why did you leave us like that, all by yourself, and not tell us? We were very worried and tried to find you." Gregorio reflected and finally related, "There was a rabbit that hopped close by me when I was on watch that night. He kept looking at me, would hop a few feet away, then hop back and look at me again. I wondered if he wanted me to follow him, so I did. He kept that up for a long time and I followed him. And I ended up here. I lost track of the rabbit when we came to the edge of that arroyo.

It looked too steep for me to climb down. I walked along the edge until I needed to lie down which I did over there under that boulder where you found me. I thought about trying to cross the canyon to climb up on that plateau several times but never did try it for some reason."

Gregorio looked up at the plateau and said, "But now that I am thinking about it, again, let's try it. What do you think, Juan?" Juan pushed his two crossed hands outward saying in a stern voice, "Absolutely not! We are not loco!"

Josie explored the lovely area surrounding the pool of fresh, spring water. She was certain that this was the area that her Grandmothers' family story had described. She called to the others, "Help me to find the line of rocks with the door space." Wandering around, kicking away small mounds of blown sand, soon enough, they located the rocks still lined up to form the bottom row of one wall and doorway of the chapel which was to be dedicated to Our Lady of Guadalupe. Josie silently told her Grandmothers, "Thank you. Help us to carry out the request of Our Lady."

Josie and the others sat around the pool with rolled up pant-legs cooling their bare feet in it. She addressed them seriously saying, "It is my belief that Our Lady's message is meant to be carried out by us, now, here in this place. There are too many coincidences not to believe it should not happen. So, with each of us helping to build it let us begin. Do you wish to help?" Eventually, all nodded, "Yes."

Diego had a talent for a design that would utilize the materials in the area: rock walls, cedar tree poles for the door, roof, and window supports, brush for the arbor roof, and fine sand for the floor. Josie wanted to include a few benches inside for sitting and praying.

Someone had started a pot of beans cooking over the campfire, with the rabbit meat that Juan and the boys had hunted earlier. They dug cattail tubers from the pool and roasted them in the fire.

Diego assigned to Juan the task of gathering cedar poles. As Juan hiked the tributary creeks which fed into the deep arroyo, he located medium and larger sized cedar trees they needed. They were at the bottoms of steep sided ravines. His only tool was a cracked-handle axe with a dull and rusty blade that one of the men had brought in his pack.

As Juan climbed downward, the smoothly worn soles on his boots slipped frequently causing him to fall and slide on his knees and backside. The air became increasing hot with the breezes remaining up above the ravines. Juan cussed to himself muttering, "Why me?"

Hacking at the base of the tough cedar trees Juan began to sweat profusely. His hands, arms, shoulders, back, and legs began to ache. Sweat dripped into his eyes and made them burn from the salt. The more difficult the task became the more irritated Juan became. Soon, he was chopping at a frenzied rate swearing at the heat, the axe, the tough cedar wood, and the "whole idea" of building a chapel. At the height of his frenzy, his anger turned into tears of frustration, then sadness, and then surrender.

Something inside of him would not let himself quit. He continued his work. His suffering gradually slowed his movements into a methodical plodding. With shear brute force and determination, he wrestled, dragged, pushed, and muscled the cedar poles up the steep sides of the ravines to the site of the chapel.

Within the combined efforts of the other men, they hefted the logs into place. The last log remaining to be lifted was the largest one. It was to serve as the keystone brace above the door. Together they struggled to inch it upwards. Gradually, each man withdrew his hold on it leaving Juan, straining to his utmost to give it a final push into its niche completing the support for the roof. The chapel was built.

Juan collapsed resting spread-eagle on the fine, cool sand inside on the chapel floor and fell asleep. Juan dreamed chaotically. His hot perspiring face took turns at turning into the hot fire of the flames of the church that he had burned, turning into the sweaty work of lifting the cedar logs, then, in relief, turning into the cool peaceful chapel where he awoke.

Lying on the sandy floor in the darkened chapel and still steeped in the feelings of his dream he realized that the fire of his anger towards the white's church had caused much destruction. He visualized the heaps of charred ruins as the black smear of his hate which was preventing everyone from having Mass and Holy Communion. Twinges of regret and sadness for how he had hurt others filled him. He realized that his hate, like theirs for his *Abuelita,* was mean and wrong, a sin. He wished that he could take back the hurt that he had caused.

His eyes looked upwards to the brush arbor roof of this new chapel. He searched the walls made of lovingly stacked stones. Exploring the cedar log beams fitted as the window and door supports, he remembered the strenuous efforts that he, and the others, had put into the building of this lovely chapel to honor Our Lady of Guadalupe.

He felt glad that he had strained and suffered as if his hardships in building-up were somehow replacing the tearing-down of the church that he had burned in his anger and hate. He felt proud of what they had built here. A wave of gratefulness that he had been a part of building this place of faith filled him, along with the smell of supper cooking and the sounds of the pleasant conversations of his friends.

By evening all was finished. They gathered in the chapel and reflected upon what had happened. Some spoke of feeling gratitude for Gregorio's rescue. Another, spoke of feeling happiness and closeness with the others from building together. Josie prayed silently to Our Lady asking if her requests had been satisfied. Josie sensed that the answer was, "not completely".

Our Lady's work here was not yet finished.

Resting on blankets spread around the campfire the star-filled sky above was keeping night watch over them. Diego rolled over and whispered to Juan, "Did you really mean it that we could go bust out my Mother and Sister from the I.C.E. detention center?" Juan answered tiredly but with an underlying strength, "Damn straight, Diego! We haven't forgotten them. And your Mom and your Sister will know that they are still 'dearly loved'."

Striving to keep his promise, sixteen-year-old Juan with his fifteen-year-old cousins, Diego, Armando, and Gregorio, wandered in the Mexican desert from March through July. They remained in the company of Josie and Miguel's group of immigrants hiding and assisting each other on their way towards the Rio Grande River border to enter the land of their dreams, the United States of America.

CHAPTER TEN-WHO LIVES NEXT DOOR?

June

Buck jumped off the Amtrak train's bottom step onto the wide cement platform at the Chestnut Street station in Philadelphia. Dressed in his blue khaki uniform, swinging his khaki duffle bag, in synch with the long strides of his "highly polished" black shoes, he located the I.C.E. Philadelphia office building located also, on Chestnut St. He entered, pulling open the bullet-proof glass front doors. He was issued a badge, dangling from a muted blue lanyard, and taken to wait outside the office of the Special Agent In Charge (SAIC) of Enforcement and Removal Operations (ERO).

SAIC Swartz told him (in a guttural German accent) that the mission here was all about Enforcement and Removal. And, at last, they were being given free rein by this administration to do whatever it took to bring in the Illegals and lots of them. In fact, the more the better, and, again, in fact, he winked, there might even be "incentives by-the-head" to fill the detention beds quotas of the contractors. He handed Buck a flashy brochure ordering, "Memorize this."

Enforcement and Removal Operations (ERO)

ERO is responsible for enforcing the nation's immigration laws and ensuring the departure of removable aliens from the United States. ***ERO uses its deportation officers to identify, arrest, and remove aliens who violate U.S. immigration law.***

Deportation officers are responsible for the transportation and detention of aliens in ICE custody to include the removal aliens to their country of origin. Deportation officers prosecute aliens for violations of U.S. immigration and criminal law, monitor cases during deportation proceedings, supervise released aliens, and remove aliens from the United States.[10]

Deportation officers operate strategically placed Fugitive Operations Teams whose function is to locate, apprehend, and remove aliens who have absconded from immigration proceedings and remain in the United States with outstanding warrants for deportation.

ERO manages the Secure Communities program which identifies removable aliens located in jails and prisons. Fingerprints submitted as part of the normal criminal arrest and booking process will automatically check both the Integrated Automatic Fingerprint Identification System (IAFIS) of the FBI's Criminal Justice Information Services (CJIS) Division and the Automated Biometric Identification System (IDENT) of the Department of Homeland Security's US-VISIT Program.

ERO was formerly known as the Office of Detention and Removal Operations (DRO).

https://www.ice.gov/management-administration/oaq
https://www.federallawenforcement.org/border-patrol/

Standing up straight, Buck, his blue eyes brightly attentive, was silently listening and watching the SAIC. Buck looked handsome with his close-cut blond hair. Swartz paused. He impassively stared at Buck, sizing up this young man, really still a boy, standing in front of him, dressed up like a Border Patrol Officer. Gradually, Swartz began to grin. "You remind me of my past. You are young. I like you. I will call you Young Buck, or, in my native way, *Jungbuk*, (rolling the g into a k sound, in the back of his throat).

"Your father arranged for you to intern here. He wants you to observe the legal system. He is wise. And, I will respect his wishes and teach you the inside ways, the ways that get things done. And you will learn from me. You will be a good boy, for your father, and for me. *Ya? Ya!"*

He motioned to an assistant telling him to check-in Buck upstairs in the overnight quarters, dismissed them with a wave of his hand, and pointed to shut his office door. Buck settled into his small, one room quarters. He stretched out in his single bed on top of its regulation-blue government-issued blanket. He felt like he had entered a surreal world of a computer video-game. He hoped that he would have those game-powers to hop up and jump over whatever came after him.

The breakfast cafeteria serving line was steaming with heartiness. The engulfing smells alone could have made a full meal. A young man in a civilian suit and tie, placed his tray down on the cafeteria table next to Buck's. He swept a disconnected handshake towards Buck saying quickly, "Hanson, Rob Hanson. Attorney, third flood, Immigration and Criminal Law. And, you?" Buck, slightly rose off his chair seat, then, tried to reply in like manner. "Buck, Buck Shepherd. Intern. Here to learn legal stuff. Don't know where or what I'm assigned to do. First day." Buck smiled hesitantly at Rob. Rob couldn't help but giggle at Buck's dubious situation.

Looking affectionately at Buck, Rob smiled gently and said, "Welcome to the world of the big-boys who get stoked by playing hard-ball with other peoples' lives." Swiftly finishing up his breakfast, Rob carried his tray, telling Buck, "Come find me. If I can help you out, I will. Good luck." Walking away, Rob pushed a thumbs-up sign back over his shoulder to Buck who wasn't used to eating that fast.

SAIC Swartz was pointing in multiple directions to multiple people who were coming in and out of his office. Buck waited in the hall watching through the office plate glass window as the people moved busily with a sense of mission. During a lull Swartz motioned for him to enter and told him, "I want you to see how we get things done here. You will accompany my staff in three areas:

Starting today, you will ride with a Patrol Officer to see how he locates and apprehends aliens. Illegal immigrants. Second, you will go with the attorneys from the Immigration and

Criminal Law Department into the jails and prisons. You'll learn how we check the fingerprint records to see if they match up with wanted illegals. That's under the Secure Communities regulations. You'll see what jerks those city, county and state bureaucrats really are. They try everything they can come up with to keep us from doing our job. But we have some tricks up our sleeves, too. And, third, you will go with the staff to remove and deport illegals. Learning how these things really work will please your father. And me."

After a thoughtful pause, Swartz changed his tone to be quieter. He stepped a bit closer to Buck. With his hand partially covering his mouth, in a slow and confidential voice, he said, "*Jungbuk*, now that you are with us, inside, like us, you will keep private what you see and hear. Many of those on the outside of I.C.E. cannot understand the scope of our mission to get rid of illegals. When our supervisors order us to carry out our mission, we do not question authority or our duty. We only do it. We take pride in protecting each other, too. You, too, will make us proud. Ya? Ya!" Swartz motioned to an assistant, telling him to take Buck over to the Patrol Department, pointing, while shutting his office door.

Passing through several halls Buck was motioned to stand against a wall. The assistant spoke privately with the Patrol Office Supervisor before leading Buck into his office. The Supervisor introduced himself to Buck, "Wilson, OIC (Officer In Charge) Charles Wilson. I understand that you are interning with us. Welcome to the Patrol Office. You are to shadow Officer Blake and to ride with him on his shift today. How about that?" As Buck was shaking his head *yes*, Wilson was leading them to the Ready Room attached to the motor pool garage.

Wilson called Blake aside, spoke privately with him, then instructed Buck to follow Blake's orders. "Whatever you do, don't get hurt in any way. Do you understand?" Buck, feeling a bit scared, answered sharply, "Yes, Sir." Blake had Buck sit beside him in the passenger seat of the powerful patrol car, a large black SUV. Buck leaned forward trying to identify the myriad devices located on the fully loaded console dash board. Office Blake barked at him, "Look, but don't touch anything."

Blake was silent as they drove. Abruptly, a loud radio-woman's voice announced, amid static, a rapid set of numbers. Blake continued to drive on non-committedly. This routine was repeated several times intermittently. Eventually, Blake pulled the patrol car into the parking lot of a donut shop. He grinned at Buck asking, "Well, what did you expect, kid?" They sat in a booth both ordering coffee and donuts which the waitress with a practiced smile muttered, "Free." She appeared to be Hispanic with a name tag that read "Juanita." She was quite pretty. Buck especially liked her straight soft black hair even wondering what it would feel like to touch. Noticing his gaze, she smiled at him.

Blake's shoulder-mounted radio set continued to issue announcements. Hearing one, he froze, listening. Quickly he grabbed his hat and rushed towards the door. Remembering his passenger he turned and sternly ordered Buck to "Stay put! I'll come back to get you."

With white powdered sugar on his lips, Buck watched Blake screech out of the parking lot with his vehicle top lights switched on streaking red and blue flashes. Buck and Juanita looked at each other. She gave him a gentle smile.

Buck wandered around the café playing the pin ball machine. Looking around he inserted a quarter into the bubble gum machine's silver knob, turned it three times, catching the gum balls rolling out into his open palm. He exchanged a few phrases in Spanish with Juanita and began to help her clear the tables.

As he would near the kitchen door, she became nervous and distracted him away from it. He became curious as to what she might be hiding behind it but could not see through the split louvered wooden doors. Finally, carrying a black plastic dishpan full of dirty coffee cups and plates he backed himself through the swinging doors into the kitchen.

He heard the yelping of several women, saw them rip off their aprons, and fling them across the room. They blurred out the back door into the alley. He wondered if they were hurt. He ran after them calling, "Do you need some help? What's wrong?"

Out of the alley onto the sidewalk, he looked up and down the street trying to spot them. He noticed that the street sign read *Chestnut*, the same street of the I.C.E. office. He saw the women's colorful skirts fluff into a doorway half way down the block. Running, adrenaline pumping, he thought, "Now I am a man on a mission!"

Buck tried to open the solid steel door, but it was firmly locked. Banging on it alerted someone inside. Slowly the lock clicked, and the door opened slightly. Shocked, Buck said, "You're a nun!" With a gentle smile she responded, "Why, yes, I am. The Order of Grey Nuns of the Sacred Heart. My name is Sister Florence. How can I help you?"

As she surveyed him, he realized what he must look like to her. He was dressed in his Border Patrol Officer clothes. He stammered that he saw some women running from the kitchen of the donut shop into this doorway and wondered if they were hurt or needed help. Sister Florence was silent looking him up and down eyeing his uniform.

It began to dawn on Buck that the women were probably Hispanic, like Juanita, working in the kitchen, hiding, and were illegal immigrants. He had probably frightened them. His uniform spoke for him. Buck began to feel embarrassed. A flush was creeping along his neck upwards over his face. He could feel its heat but was unable to stop the flowing color as he stood before this nun. She saw everything, too.

Buck stepped back. Looking into the nun's clear green eyes he quietly said, "Will you please give the women my apologies for scaring them? I'm sorry for bothering you. Thank you." He slowly hesitated. Finally, Sister Florence said, "Would you like to come in and visit our convent's Family Service Center?

With a bit of hesitation, he followed her inside. Sister handed him a pamphlet describing their mission's services:

"Asylee Women Enterprise (A.W.E.) is a joint project of a number of Communities of Women Religious. Among the founding group are the Benedictine Sisters of Baltimore, Grey Nuns of the Sacred Heart, Mission Helpers of the Sacred Heart, School Sisters of Notre Dame, Sister of Notre Dame de Namur, Sisters of St. Joseph of Chestnut Hill, Philadelphia, Sisters of Bon Secours, Sisters of St. Francis of Philadelphia and Sisters of Mercy.
*Asylee Women Enterprise helps women seeking asylum to rebuild their lives and their spirits. Asylee Women Enterprise (AWE) provides transitional housing, companionship and community to **women seeking asylum** by offering a safe and nurturing home, opportunities to connect with women in the larger community and each other."*
https://www.greynun.org/what-we-do/advocacy/asylee-womens-enterprise-a-w-e/

At the end of the tour, Sister Florence added, "There is another important organization, The U. S. Catholic Council of Bishops which provides education about the historical circumstances leading individuals to seek asylum. The Council also offers information on immigration and criminal law that affects those individuals.

"Buck, you might wish to learn more about them, too." She offered him another pamphlet (www.usccb.org/mrs Migration and Refugee Service Office of Migration Policy and Public Affairs). She ended his tour back at the front door graciously opening it for him.

Buck was thoroughly touched by stepping into the convent's world of compassion. Tears trickled down his face as he walked back to the donut shop. He was so happy to know of the existence of such a place and of people who operated it. He hoped that Diego's mother and sister might be in a similar place.

Back at the café, Buck was sitting in the booth sipping a glass of milk when Officer Blake drove up. Buck ran out when he heard the honk of the SUV's horn. During the ride in the patrol car back to the station he was quiet, thinking of the visit with the nun. Officer Blake had dirt and leaves on the front of his uniform. Blake roughly explained with pride in his tone, "I'm on the Fugitive Operations Team that just picked up three aliens on a rural road west of the city, in Berks County. The wetbacks work at mushroom and chicken farms out there. Of course, they ran when they saw us coming with our flashing lights and, of course, we chased them. We brought 'em down! The scum!" Smiling, he brushed at the front of his uniform. Buck wondered what had actually happened. He felt a bit overwhelmed by the violence that he guessed had taken place. The silence was comforting. Nothing was shared about his visit to the convent.

The next day he was told to report to the legal office on the third floor. Buck wandered, lost, down the hall. Rob Hanson waved at him to enter his office. They both felt glad to see each other. Rob offered Buck a soda and motioned him to a chair next to his behind a large desk. A map was spread out on the desk. Touching his finger to a spot located on Chestnut Street he said, "We are here and we are going over here to the Philadelphia city jail. There we hope to compare our list of aliens with the jail's list of inmates. This is allowed under a DHS (Department of Homeland Security) program called Secure Communities. The program is supposed to prevent us at I.C.E. from apprehending the illegals while they are under the jurisdiction of other legal organizations. This includes such organizations as jails, courthouses, prisons, schools, hospitals, etc. The illegals are off limits to us until they step out of the doors and onto public sidewalks. Then we can arrest them!

"However, there seems to be a territorial conflict. I.C.E. interprets the regulations to allow the Border Patrol Officers to apprehend aliens almost anywhere. The other organizations try to keep from losing control of the aliens and block I.C.E. personnel wherever they can."

Buck wondered, "Why is it so important to all of them as to *who* is actually capturing the illegal aliens, Rob?"

Rob smiled at Buck. "Very perceptive question. I see that you are a thinker. Now since I see that I will educate you about what is really going on with all of the immigration regulations, legislation, and, the blocking of certain legislative reform. This is public knowledge, on the record, but many politicians try to hide and minimize the background context of this information. Which is, briefly stated, whoever is holding a captured illegal alien for the day gets paid the lucrative government contract for his room and board. All funded by the manipulated, working class, U.S. citizens' taxes. The old adage, saying, 'Follow the money,' certainly holds true with trying to understand the immigration issue."

By now Buck was curious about the next twist to the story but he was restless, too. Seeing him fidget, Rob picked up his brief case and they headed for the jail. Upon arriving, Buck anticipated that they would walk up and down the jail corridors viewing the inmates behind bars like in the zoo. But Rob pushed the elevator button to the second floor. Finding the Records Office, the busy staff directed them to an alcove with hard metal folding chairs at a grey steel table, too small for all their paper work. They struggled to read hundreds of inmates' microfiche records and links to their fingerprints, most of which were over two years old. The jail employees giggled at their discomfort. After about fifteen minutes, Rob stood up and they left.

Riding in their black SUV agency car driving slowly through traffic, Buck asked, "Rob, what was all that about back there?" Rob didn't hesitate to explain. "The DHS program called Secure Communities requires the jails, courts, etc. to allow I.C.E. access to information, including fingerprints, that might identify illegal aliens especially those who have criminal charges against them. But the jails, courts, prisons, etc. want to get paid through government contracts to house the alien per day in their beds for as long as possible. So, they make it difficult to release them to anyone else or to allow the suspects to wear an ankle tracking device and remain free.

"The cities' organizations half-heartedly agree to notify I.C.E. when the illegals are released, although it rarely happens in fact, due to various excuses. And I.C.E. is not allowed to actually apprehend aliens while they are within public buildings, inside jails, courthouses, etc. but they can arrest them as soon as they step off those properties.

"You have probably already observed, Buck, that many law enforcement and military personnel in all countries take a certain group pride in acting tough, bullying, defending their local sources of income. That's income like fines, property seizures, bribes, pay-offs, and contracts for bed quotas within their assigned territories. Many believe that they are above the law in times of emergency and at most other times, too. Their basic training teaches them to expect the deadliest and worst of everyone. They are scared into taking an attitude of shoot-before-you-are shot. So be careful. Also, they are sometimes faced with having to deal with dangerous and violent criminals."

CHAPTER ELEVEN-WHO LIVES IN BERKS COUNTY?

July

Picking up fast-food meals and eating in the car, their destination was the Management Unit of I.C.E.'s Berks County Family Detention Center, the Juvenile and Family Residential Center. Rob informed Buck that they were driving about ninety miles northwest to Leesburg, Pennsylvania. Their instructions were to locate a one Rosa de la Vasquez and transport her back to Philadelphia to place her on a plane for deportation back to El Salvador. Rob explained: "Our legal office examined every court order and appeal that her private attorney had filed for her to be declared an Asylum Seeker, not an Illegal Immigrant, but all were denied yesterday by an Immigration Judge."

Stunned into silence, Buck began to sniffle then cried out loud for about a minute. Rob, too, silently began clearing his throat and making frequent swallows. In a painfully cracked voice, Buck blurted, "She might be my friend's mom, too! I just hate this." He loudly slurped his fast food drink sucking the straw and shaking the ice in his empty soda cup. Underneath his noisy slurping anger, he had heard something new in his voice. It had slipped up and down alternating between a boyish weakness and a deep manly strength. He couldn't help it. A smile stretched over his tear-streaked cheeks as he looked out the side car window at the scenery whizzing by. He suddenly remembered, "My fifteenth birthday is in four days. On July the 4th!" He knew that everything was going to be different. His changing voice meant that he was no longer just a little kid. He could *do* things. On his own.

Their SUV tires crunched over the parking lot gravel. Buck scanned the appearance of the imprinted, red, brick concrete which covered the institutional buildings. Its pretend family home decorations gave him the creeps. He did not want to go inside, feeling it was secretly like a spider-web-type trap. Walking through the entrance doors and seeing the dorm rooms filled with moms and kids, he felt the impulse to rush through the halls and to yell desperately, "Diego's mom and sister, are you here?"

Buck and Rob were seated in a small parlor on wooden, straight-back, heavy pine chairs pulled up to a scuffed up matching table. They waited for the unfortunate inmate, one Rosa de la Vasquez, to be brought to them for deportation.

The matron, with a hand on Rosa's upper arm, guided her in and seated her at the table. The matron stepped into the hall to stand impassively outside the open door. Rob and Buck rose and extended their handshakes but the thin, short woman declined to touch them. "Hi, Rosa. I'm Rob and this is Buck, an intern. We're with I.C.E. legal department." Sitting down they all looked at each other. Dressed in a tan scrubs uniform, Rosa's quick black eyes took in both of them. They felt sized up by someone well-experienced in needing to protect herself from any surprise attacks or tricks. Sitting very still she was tensely expectant and remained silent. Rob broke the silence with a slight clearing of his throat.

Using his flat voice, he looked her in the eyes and said quietly, "Rosa, the last of the appeals filed by your attorney to grant you asylum status have been rejected. I'm sorry. You are to come with us to the airport in Philadelphia to be deported back to El Salvador. The matron has your things in a sack for you. We are ready to leave now." Rob rose, scraping back his heavy wooden chair.

Rosa startled in shock. Faster than Buck ever saw anyone move, she darted through the door. The agile matron grabbed Rosa around the waist from behind and pushed her face down on the vinyl floor of the hall, knee on her back. The matron pulled out a syringe and pushed a shot of muscle relaxant medication into Rosa's butt. Rosa wiggled violently, screaming hysterically, "Mari! Mari! I can't leave without her!"

As they watched the painful scene from the doorway, Rob and Buck looked at each other, in shock. Calling out to the matron with some urgency in his voice, Rob said, "Wait! Who is Mari?" The matron was wrestling Rosa back into her chair, and informed Rob: "That's her three-year old daughter."

Beginning to wilt in her chair and between muffled sobs, Rosa explained: "Two years ago, in El Salvador, the drug cartels killed my husband and said they would be back to kidnap my son and make him join their gang. My father had also been killed. My mother told me to *run*. To save us, my twelve-year-old son and Mari and I hiked from El Salvador through Mexico to the Texas border. Near the border we had to pay a coyote' who put us in life jackets and pulled us with a rope across the Rio Grande River into Texas in the dark of the night. When the sun came up, the Border Patrol officers rode their horses and chased us down in the bushes along the river at La Grulla. But they couldn't find my son. He got away.

"They marched us to a black SUV and drove us to Dilly Family Detention Center in Texas near McAllen. We were there about nine months then they transferred us to Karnes Family Detention Center south of San Antonio. We were there for about a year until they transferred us here to Pennsylvania, to Berks.

About three months ago an immigration judge ruled that I was being charged as a dangerous *criminal* for crossing the border with my daughter. That's when they took Mari away. A month later they told me she was in a shelter but didn't know which one."

Rosa began to occasionally slur some of her words as the injected muscle relaxant began to affect her. She continued telling her story in a semi-detached tone interspersed with sobbing.

"The Immigration Judge ordered Mari, my Mariposa, my butterfly, to be 'removed' from me. I don't understand why. How could anyone do that? Take a three-year-old child from her mother? And she was so scared and couldn't stop crying."

By now, everyone's emotions were just too painful. Rob left the room. Buck followed. Rosa continued to wilt, laying her head on the table, and to sob on and off. The matron settled into a chair by the door and relaxed into a waiting mode. She thought,

65

"Another day at work. How many of these cases have I seen? They don't pay me enough for this."

Rob was outdoors sitting on a bench beside a small hybrid tree which had been bred to grow a small round ball of foliage for conformity and low maintenance. Its essential tree-ness of wide-spreading arms and dense leaves had been genetically engineered away depriving hot and tired travelers of its refreshing shade. Gone, too, was its inspiring loveliness so needed by those suffering in this place of capture.

Buck had walked in the opposite direction on the sidewalk. He leaned against the building wall in the shade. He watched Rob trying to figure out what to do now that Rosa's kid was in the soup with them. He thought, "Kids and moms." He remembered his own mom. He felt a crushing need in his chest for her to hug him and stroke back his hair like she used to when he was a kid. His throat began to tighten and his eyes to water. He took out his cell phone and dialed home. She answered. Hearing her familiar voice triggered his flow of tears. "Hi, Mom. I was wanting you to hug me, like we used to…." They finally said good-bye and hung up.

Buck slowly walked over to Rob's bench and sat next to him. Rob was silent looking around and up towards the distant Appalachian Mountains. Buck said, "Rob, why did they take Mari away from Rosa?" Rob began to explain the rules. His factual tone of voice was weakened with an underlying sadness. "When someone enters the U.S. without proper papers such as a visa or green card, the laws recently have been changed so that now they are committing a *criminal act* not a civil infraction. This is how Rosa is charged under *criminal law*, not civil law.

"When someone is charged under criminal law instead of civil law, she is not allowed to have custody of a child, as she is considered dangerous, a criminal. And she must be locked up, not allowed to be free on bond or only wearing an electronic surveillance cuff on her ankle.

"In cases such as Rosa's, by law the child must have an appointed guardian for the safety of the child. So, in this case, the Immigration Court Judge appointed the U.S. Department of Human Services (US DHS) to be Mari's guardian. They in turn, placed Mari in a licensed child welfare facility somewhere. Probably in Chicago, as those facilities are frequently used in these cases. Or the ones in New York."

Buck asked, "How can we get Rosa and Mari back together?"

Rob turned away looking at the blue skies high above the Appalachian Mountains. "It's impossible. Legally."

Sitting passively on the bench, Buck felt a building sense of despair in the pit of his stomach for not being able to save Rosa and Mari. That despair became a limpness in his arms as he tried to lift his right arm. Was it becoming paralyzed? He held it out horizontally intending to comment on its flabby feeling. Instead, his words squeaked out in a garbled deep baritone of a young man's changing voice. Startled, then reminded of his rising manhood he saw that his arm was not flabby at all. He flexed his bicep, smiling. Impulsively, he stepped up on the bench, stretching himself upwards onto his tip-toes, flexing both biceps. Out came a loud Tarzan call to the sky.

Rob jerked his head to look at Buck. Watching him enjoy his newly discovered coming-of-age strength, Rob grinned, remembering his own time so long ago.

As Rob and his "dangerous criminal" Rosa climbed into the car, Buck visualized himself as Mighty Mouse, mentally wrapping his cape around his shoulder. He jumped into the back seat to sit beside Rosa, hoping, perchance, to pull off a *rescue.*

Rob and Rosa were quiet. Buck was talkative. He began telling Rosa about his good friends Juan Diego, Armando and Gregorio. But not about the part of burning down the church. Buck wondered out loud where the boys were now. He told her about *Abuela,* and the priest refusing her communion. How Juan gave her the Our Lady of Guadalupe candle. And how she died. He shared with Rosa how he visited Juan's mother on his bike and how she wondered where her sister-in-law, Diego's mom and her little daughter were. Buck added that Juan said he and his *primo* were going to find his mom and "bust her out." Rosa was withdrawn, listening to his non-stop talking only responding non-verbally to parts of his story.

Suddenly, Buck froze. He looked closely at Rosa. She returned his intense look. He gasped and whispered ever so softly, "Why, *you* are Diego's mom, aren't you? And your little girl, Mari, is his little sister! And Diego is your son that hid from the Border Patrol, then lived with Juan's family, his *primo*! And, now I've found you! We've got to tell Diego!"
Buck grabbed Rosa's arm and hands, squeezing them and laughing in happiness. She returned his squeezing and laughed with him.

Rob kept his eyes on the highway, watching the mile markers zip past as they neared the Philadelphia airport. Buck and Rosa began to jabber to each other in Spanish, smiling and giggling. Rob guessed that they were making plans on how to escape. And they were. Rob had briefly thought about how he could let Rosa escape. But knew that he couldn't get away with it. His career with I.C.E. would be over. He might even be put in jail. He considered that he would wait. Wait and watch what those two would come up with then make his decisions.

Exiting onto Chestnut Street Rob announced that he needed to stop at the office to pick up Rosa's airplane tickets. During the slow drive in heavy traffic along Chestnut, Buck enthusiastically asked Rob if he would stop at the donut shop. Buck said that the least they could do was to give Rosa some donuts to take with her on the plane.

Rob, looking in the rearview mirror at Buck's transparent face acted a bit reluctant then said "Okay." Buck and Rosa squeezed hands. Turning into the parking lot Rob stopped in a space that had a full view through a plate glass window of the inside of the shop. Buck opened his car door and said to Rob, "Rosa has to come, too, to pick out her favorite donuts, okay?"
Rob rolled his eyes thinking, "How dumb do they think I am?"
All at once, a loud screeching of tires grabbed their attention. Rob glanced into his rear-view mirror. He watched as a huge

black SUV with flashing police lights crashed into his rear bumper sending his car through the plate glass window.

A drunk Officer Blake rolled out from the hole where his driver's side-door had flown off. He passed out, falling onto the parking lot and breaking his arm. His black SUV's flashing lights continued to streak red and blue until the car battery eventually ran down. An ambulance with its flashing lights carried him at top speed to the hospital.

Rob had hit his forehead on the steering wheel which raised a wide bump-of-a-bruise of many colors. Buck kneeled beside him until the ambulance arrived to deliver him to the hospital emergency room. Unhurt, Buck stayed with him in the hospital overnight.

Rosa was nowhere to be found.

The next morning at I.C.E. headquarters Rob, suffering with a throbbing headache, was sitting quietly at his desk on the third floor. On the first floor near the patrol vehicle area Blake sat subdued in a cubicle with one arm in a sling. On his desk top his other elbow was holding his head in his hand. Blake was still hung over.

Deep in thought Buck was lingering in the cafeteria. Sitting alone at a table in the corner slowly stirring his second cup of milk-and-sugar-loaded coffee, he was startled by someone bumping the table. Buck looked up then jumped up and hugged his brother, William. He held onto his big brother's chest so tightly that he squeezed tears from both of them.

William looked his little brother up and down glad to have found him again. "Mom called and asked me to bring you home. At least, for a while, if that's okay with you. Dad said it was okay with him, too." Buck felt a surge of love for his family and was ready to go right away. Then he remembered Rosa and a cloud of worry came over his face.

He searched William's face wondering if he should tell him about the rescue plan that he and Rosa had concocted. Would William turn them in? He felt a bit scared, realizing that now his brother was an I.C.E. Border Patrol Officer whose mission it was to "apprehend and detain" people like Rosa. But wait, William was not wearing his uniform, just his civvies jeans and a tee shirt. Buck blurted, "William, where is your uniform?" William, smiling, said, "I don't need it anymore. I quit. I want to go build something. Are you about ready to go home with me?" Grinning, Buck said, "I need to do a few things first. Can I meet you at the donut shop later? And I need your help with some stuff, okay?" William nodded, yes, as Buck rushed away.

Buck took the stairs two at a time balancing in one hand a paper plate piled high with a freshly baked German apple strudel pastry. He stood outside Swartz's office waiting respectfully. Finally, Swartz sternly waved for him to enter. Buck waited for him to speak. Swartz scowled. Buck silently offered the delicious smelling pastry to him. With his hesitant smile, Buck also offered his apologies for the problems at the donut shop. Looking at the pastry Swartz finally took it from Buck, sat down at his desk, and began to slowly eat it savoring the treat. Buck remained respectfully standing and quiet.

Obviously, taking the time to think, Swartz finally told Buck, "You must learn from this a lesson that I will teach you: It is sometimes better to say nothing about incidents. For example, very bad it could be to others, the public and superior, by pointing out the image of our officers being drunk, wrecking expensive department cars, damaging a private business building, losing track of a prisoner, and all of this taking place at a donut shop A place where officers should not be while on duty. Do you understand how bad this could be, *Jungbuk?"*

Buck replied sharply, "Yes, Sir, OIC Swartz!"
Swartz leaned forward towards Buck and cautioned him with a wagging finger, "Then, do you agree that this incident probably did not happen, and that you know almost nothing about it?"

Buck again replied, "Yes, Sir, OIC Swartz!"

Swartz, said in a hearty tone, "Good, *Jungbuk.* You are learning well in your internship. I have taught you well. I am proud of you. Oh, and your father called and wants you to return to him so that he can teach you more. So, you are dismissed from

70

my command. Go gather your gear. And remember all that you have learned from me about how to carry out your duties with pride and honor, *ya? Ya!*" Buck, looking him directly in eyes, gave him an awkward salute. Hesitantly, Buck rounded the desk and hugged the large waist of OIC Swartz good-bye. Swartz grinned and patted him on the back, muttering, "Good boy, *Jungbuk*, good boy."

Buck ran up the stairs two at a time to the third floor. Poor Rob was sitting tiredly at his desk shuffling papers. Buck put his head through the door. Rob waved him to enter then to sit. Buck told him briefly about what Swartz had said about the "incident" and Rob smiled weakly, relieved. He said, "So, I guess, I have to do nothing about apprehending Rosa. And sometimes people do get lost in the system. Even some computer files have been known to disappear, somehow deleted. Accidents and machine errors do happen, sometimes.

"And, Buck, if you happen to see Rosa, you can tell her that her records will be deleted from the system. But, unfortunately, legally, there is nothing that we can do for her child. Mari is now in the system program of guardianship of the Office of Refugee Resettlement (ORR) under the jurisdiction of the Department of Homeland Security. And the laws have been changed in such ways that there is no legal path for her ever to be returned to her mother. The usual result is that Mari will remain in custody of an organization in a shelter which has a federal contract to be paid, usually $162.00 per bed per day. They will collect money on her until she reaches the age of eighteen. Tell Rosa that I am sorry." Buck thanked Rob for all his help and they said their good-byes.

Buck ran down the stairs two at a time back to the cafeteria. He bought a bottle of tomato juice, some aspirin, and a glazed donut. He hurried up the stairs to Blake's cubicle. Seeing him suffering and looking like he needed to vomit, Buck entered and softly set down the refreshments on the desk in front of Blake. Blake barely raised his eyes. Half grinning, he gently pushed away the donut. Blake raised the bottle of tomato juice in a crooked toast to Buck. Smiling good-bye at him, Buck left.

Gathering his gear, he changed into his civilian jeans and tee shirt with an image of a sparkling mountain lake on the back. He folded his border patrol uniform and left it on the cot. He thought, "It was getting too small for me, anyway." Buck took the stairs two at a time and hurried down the sidewalk along Chestnut Street to the donut shop.

CHAPTER TWELVE-WHO LIVES IN CHICAGO?

July

Meeting up with William sitting at a booth in the donut shop and enjoying a toasted coconut donut, Buck shared his story. He excitedly explained to William the situation with rescuing Rosa. Hoping for a supportive reaction, Buck asked William if he would accompany him down the street to the Grey Nuns Family Center to join Rosa. Buck so hoped that she had safely made it there and was following their rescue plan.

William said that he did not want to do anything illegal. Buck offered that Rosa was no longer registered in the I.C.E. computer system. Considering this information William added that now she would be needing some identification papers. They continued to discuss possible problems they might be facing as they walked down the sidewalk. Knocking on the door of the Grey Nuns center, once again, Sister Florence welcomed them.

Sister Florence invited them to sit in the activity room where several of the women residents were studying on computers and Rosa was being counselled by a priest. Sister Florence said to Buck, "Come with me. I would like to introduce you to the Senior Assistant of the US Catholic Council of Bishops, Office of Immigration Refugees, Father Benito."

Seeing him up close, Buck and William said in unison, "Father Benito!" William reminded the priest, "You used to be our parish priest." Father Benito remembered them recalling what a good job William had performed as his "altar boy."

Buck eagerly shared with Rosa and Father Benito the results of the car accident and that OIC Schwartz and Rob had deleted her immigration records. But that her daughter, Mari, continued to be in the system of ORR, probably in a shelter in Chicago, with virtually no legal path to be reunited with her Mother. William said that Rosa would be needing some identification papers.

Sister Florence turned to Father Benito, looking expectantly at him. He was silent. She said to Buck, William, and Rosa, "Do as he tells you." She left them, walking away to assist the other women.

Buck spoke enthusiastically to Father Benito, "Father, you remember Rosa's family in your Spanish parish, don't you? Diego is her son! Juan's mother is her sister-in-law!" Father Benito stared impassively at the floor.

Buck continued, energetically, "We have to drive to Chicago and rescue Mari! Then we have to drive them back to our town in Texas, so their family can be all together again. Can you drive us in your car?"

William, Buck, Rosa, and Sister Florence, from across the room, all froze. They looked intensely expectant at Father Benito who began to clear his throat loudly and squirm.

Father Benito excused himself "to go to the chapel to pray", and quickly left the room. Sister Florence quickly followed him down the hall which led to the chapel and to the back door. As he was pushing open the backdoor bar handle to exit, Sister Florence grabbed his cassock sleeve and pulled him backwards and into the chapel. She maneuvered him into sitting down in the corner of a pew.

Their voices drifted down the hall. The others could hear them sometimes arguing rather loudly, sometimes quietly pleading, sometimes desperately demanding. They heard Sister's soft crying and the reasonable insistences of Father. Then there was only silence.

The others felt the desperate importance of what was being decided in the chapel. They guessed that the silence meant that Sister Florence and Father Benito were praying. So, the others, too, began to pray silently. Some kneeled and some sat while others stood looking out the window. Buck was hoping for a miracle.

As Sister Florence remained kneeling and praying in the chapel, Father walked back into the room. He announced matter-of-factly to Buck, William, and Rosa: "Load up your things in the car. It is the black Lincoln parked in the alley by the back door. We're leaving in fifteen minutes to *rescue* our Mari in Chicago."

He then spoke in a loud voice down the hall to the chapel, "God willing. And Sister Florence willing." Kneeling in the chapel, Sister Florence heard him loud and clear. A huge smile spread over her tear-stained cheeks.

William was the chauffer. Rosa sat next to him. In the backseat Buck sat silently admiring the tree-covered Appalachian Mountains. Father Benito sat with his open computer on his lap. Engrossed in a website search trying to locate Mari, he finally exclaimed, "I've found her! She's in the Chicago shelter operated by our USCCB's Immigrant Children's Program. That's very fortunate. I have some hierarchical authority over her placement. Now, to figure out how to justify an intervention."

Rosa was elated, if a bit doubtful and suspicious. She decided to stay quiet, observing what these *gringos* were going to do. She had learned to be hyper-vigilant, always watching for escape routes knowing that it wasn't safe to trust anyone. Her priority, as always, was to find and keep her daughter with her at any price. Having no family, she wanted to fade out of sight, be unnoticed and on the move when necessary, to work and live safely wherever she could in the US.

And she desperately hoped that her son was figuring out how to do that, somewhere, too. She had a deep-seated fear that never left her that her son had been captured into the I.C.E. detention system as she had been for these last two years. Feelings of despair for his possible loss of freedom haunted her at night, exhausting her to the bone that no amount of sleep could relieve. She sank into feelings of hopelessness, giving up on ever finding her precious son again.

She felt deep shame like she was committing the mortal sin of motherhood as she let go of the emotional life line to her son. Riding in this expensive car, swaying with its speeding rhythm, and listening to its tires whining as they crossed bridges, it was becoming more difficult for her to even remember his beloved face.

Taking turns driving through the night, they entered Chicago on highway I-90 during the morning rush-hour traffic. Father Benito rented a room at the Eldridge Hotel near Lake Michigan and Lake Shore Drive. They took turns showering, napping, and eating meals downstairs in the café. Father Benito spent the day at the local office of the shelter announcing that he had arrived from the national office of the USCCB to make a resident transfer of one Mariposa de la Vasquez to another shelter. He ended the visit stating that he would return the next day and pick up the child for transport to another shelter.

Father Benito left the building and drove through Melrose Park and over to his familiar Italian home neighborhood. He parked at his relative's supper club in Elmwood near Harlem St. and Grand Ave. His uncle, two cousins, and three aunts greeted him boisterously and served him his favorite home cooked pasta with wine from Sicily. After much visiting he sat with his uncle at the private family table.

His uncle Salvi asked him, "How are you progressing on your career path with the bishops? Can we call you, 'Monsignor" yet?" Benito said, "No, not yet, Uncle. The church moves slowly on these things, you know." Salvi, with exasperation, countered back, "What do we need to do then nephew? More money to the Council?" "Benito looked discouraged and shook his head, no. "What then? How about you building a church or setting up an orphanage, something to prove how powerful you can be, something to command the respect of those church bureaucrats? What do you want to do, Benito? Tell me, my favorite brother's son. Remember, you are part of The Family. We want to be proud of you. Our Family would be proud to have a Bishop! Tell me how much money you need to build your church and orphanage? And then we can all attend the dedication ceremony to celebrate with you!"

Benito sheepishly lowered his head. He quietly admitted that he did need a favor. "Uncle, I am still working with these immigrant families. Could you supply me with fake identification and legal papers for a mother and her child? I am transporting them from Chicago tomorrow and taking them to Texas."

Salvi smiled knowingly at Benito's "irregular" methods, saying, "It is good that you have not forgotten your roots in our Family. We do what must be done, eh?" Benito and Salvi hugged each other hard. His relatives stood inside the club's front window and waved good-bye to him. His shiny black Lincoln sedan made an impressive exit through the narrow streets bringing a smile to his uncle's face.

Early the next morning, after receiving the requested "papers" from his uncle, Benito and his gang slowly drove through downtown Chicago traffic in the large shiny black Cadillac. Acting like seasoned calm bank robbers they successfully "rescued" Mari from the children's shelter. With Rosa holding Mari on her lap, the child and her mother glued themselves to each other during the two-day journey. They eventually arrived at their destination, deep in the heart of Texas.

CHAPTER THIRTEEN-DOWN IN TEXAS

July

After checking his flock into a motel, Father Benito took an Uber to Woodlawn Avenue arriving at the office of the Catholic Archdiocese Office for a collegial discussion. Being shown into the office of an assistant, Father Benito inquired about the archbishop's interest in working with the USCCB in establishing within his archdiocese an Immigrant Project. The archbishop's assistant was uncomfortable with the idea and spoke of the current unrest and attitudes of the established white members of his diocese who, incidentally, contributed substantially to the diocese. Immigration was a subject that sparked strong negative emotions and hostilities among many Catholics here.

In a patronizing tone he briefly explained and defended the resistance of some Traditional Catholics to changing and upsetting the long-held societal entitlement status levels of several ethnic classes. "You must understand, Father, that a large segment of the archdiocese is Hispanic. However most of the current contributing Catholics in this area have an ancestral loyalty identification with the white European (the German, the Polish, the Irish) Catholic traditions, not with the Hispanic Central American Catholic culture. They are quite different, you know, within the languages, the music, the art, images, levels of education, types of employment, and levels of social class and wealth. For example, during the season of Advent and Christmas the Traditional Catholics' preferences are for German carols and snowy Alps manger scenes and legends like St. Nicholas, not *pinatas*."

Father Benito agreed saying, "That was the situation that I found myself in when I served as the pastor at a parish in a small town located about one hundred and fifty miles west of here. I left shortly after the main parish church building burned down. I then found a job in Washington D.C. with the USCCB. Formerly, when I was in that west Texax town, we maintained a small church for the Hispanics. Their Catholicism is definitely culturally different.from European Catholics"

The assistant nodded his head in agreement. "Yes, the Hispanics are superstitious with their irrational emotional devotion to the images and shrines of Our Lady of Guadalupe. They are embarrassing in the way some of them grovel on their knees instead of walking while making pilgrimages or even within the parish churches when approaching communion.

"They are too fearful of everything and won't think for themselves. For example, on their own they won't quietly use birth control and abortion to plan their families like the white traditional Catholics are reasonably doing in secret. Not using effective birth control keeps the Hispanics, especially the women, oppressed and poor, never being able to get out of poverty. Most of the priests privately know and support birth control and divorce knowing that they are necessary at times. But our priests must publicly avoid saying so to keep their jobs. We see the suffering of the Hispanic families, especially, the women. And privately, we wish that they would use their intelligence and gumption to choose to do what is best for themselves and their families just quietly and not ask the church if it's alright.

"And the same goes for the many of our people who are born gay. We wish that they would quietly stand up for themselves and just go ahead and do what they know is best and loving for themselves and their partners and their kids and families. I think that God wants them to do that too. It's the loving thing to do. But they don't stand up for themselves, do they?

"They're waiting on Rome. Maybe someday Rome will change. But I understand. It takes courage to be true to who we are. Personally, I look to the women though. They can be fierce when it comes to going after what is needed for their children and families. Mama bears!

"To protect the conventional cultural comfortableness of the whites, there is the tendency to divide religious liturgies and service programs into separate parishes and programs. For

79

example, the cathedral (and most of the other parish churches')
culture and monetary contributions reflect the European
Catholic traditions primarily. While in other usually poorer
sections of the city and counties, we have set up additional
facilities for the Hispanics.

"So, what I am trying to let you know, no offense to anyone
implied, is that in trying to keep the archdiocese financially
stable and peaceful, and contributions flowing in an orderly
fashion, the hierarchy does not want to stir up controversy or to
risk offending the whites by diverting any funds and missionary
support to the dark-skinned Hispanics and their unpopular and
even hated illegal immigrants.

"And another very important provision here is that the
archdiocese must have full ownership and title to all land and
capital assets of all Catholic enterprises, missions, outreach
programs, as well as properties and lands of monasteries,
seminaries, convents, chapels, churches, parishes, including any
new shelters. All properties.

"And of course, the Archdiocese is always promoting some
fundraising initiative so any competing fundraising initiatives by
other Catholic projects for their own goals is discouraged, if not
prohibited. I'm sure you understand the fiscal necessities of this,
right?

Father Benito and the archbishop's assistant shared a long
eye-to-eye look. They were communicating that they understood
each other. All too well. After a long period of consideration,
Father Benito said, "I too grew up in neighborhoods of
conflicting ethnic groups. My Sicilian family was not loved in
most other neighborhoods in Chicago. My family and I quickly
adjusted by learning to be loyal and to help out each other within
the Family. It meant our survival." Father Benito paused.
Looking meaningfully at the assistant he added in a strong and
serious tone, "And, the *Family* that I belong to continues to take
care of each other today no matter who or where we are or who
we are dealing with."

Listening carefully the assistant paused then jerked his head and looked intensely at Father Benito. His frightened expression revealed that he had just understood that Benito was communicating to him that the Archdiocese was now dealing with a member of a powerful Mob Family.

He stood up and leaned over his desk respectfully extending his hand to shake Father Benito's hand and said, "Well Father thank you for informing us of what plans you might be having. When you get the specifics mapped out, let me know how we can assist you, okay? Let's see what can be worked out for the good of everyone, okay? And you know how we administrators are about always needing and shuffling around the money as it's up to us to make sure that the organization keeps its doors open, right? I'll work with you Father since you understand our situation too. Perhaps, we could help each other in friendly ways? After all we all are in the same church business, right?" They concluded with both being pleased with their meeting.

Father Benito felt drained but at the same time he felt challenged. An unfamiliar spurt of interest and energy began to percolate within him. Stepping out of the cavernous atmosphere of the archdiocesan business building into the bright cheerful sunlight, he called Uber to drive him to the downtown River District. Finding an outdoor black wrought-iron table and chair overlooking the slow-flowing river he ordered himself a fine white Italian wine. Sipping it, he dialed his cell phone ringing up Sister Florence back in Philadelphia.

Hearing the calmness in her gentle voice he asked, "Well, Sister, were you in the chapel discussing with God what I am to do next?" with a soft chuckle. Her smile came through. "Why yes I was. And God explained the whole thing to me. And he even told me to be in charge of telling you what to do." Benito laughed and began to wish that she were here with him.

In a mockingly serious tone he said, "Sister, in my USCCB role of giving you and your organization *advice and counsel*" for the mission, I am *counseling* you to come to Texas to explore possible placements for a re-united family of an immigrant mother and her child. And I am *advising* you to fly out here tomorrow because I need to figure out soon what to do with Rosa and Mari." Sister Florence was quiet. Benito added, "Oh, and Sister. Please?" She replied with a slight banter, "Well let me ask God about it and I'll get back to you." He said, "Use my credit card for the plane ticket and whatever you will need." And he gave her the card number.

That night in his dreams Father Benito was traveling through the old familiar streets of his childhood neighborhood in Chicago. Sitting on their porches, standing in their doorways, resting on their steps, his relatives and neighborhood friends were smiling at him, waving and calling out encouraging phrases in Italian to him. He felt a family connection course through him. He felt brave and pleased that they approved of him. He felt included in the community and a strong loyalty to The Family.

He waved back and smiled at them, acknowledging and accepting their shared hopes for his future successes. He felt strengthened with their familiar family energy. He felt that he was not alone in his work. He wanted to keep moving and to produce something to make them proud of him. He was aware of soaking up a richness of rest that was transforming him. He surrendered willingly into the arms of sleep.

Father Benito pulled his black Cadillac up to the airport terminal curb as Sister Florence walked out of the terminal's sliding glass doors, pulling her small suitcase. They caught each other's eyes and smiled spontaneously. As the large black Cadillac weaved them away from the airport amid the exiting shuttles, cabs and cars, they both spoke at once jabbering as fast as they could. They both had so much to say. Suddenly they became aware of their shared excitement and stopped speaking feeling slightly embarrassed at their feelings of closeness and happiness.

Looking out her side window Sister Florence wondered how she could immediately return to the terminal and catch a flight back to her convent. Benito wondered how quickly he could drive to the motel and let her out. They both remained silent wondering what they should do. Father Benito abruptly shifted his position sitting up straighter.

Resuming his self-control and using his deepest matter-fact-tone Benito stated, "I have a plan to establish an orphanage or children's shelter and to build a church. I have already contacted the archbishop's office about putting the shelter within this diocese. I think that I can get them to allow me full rein." Pausing, Benito continued in a monotone. Rising up within him was the embarrassing feeling that he was the penitent and Sister Florence was the priest hearing his confession. His elated feelings had deflated. He was realizing the dishonor of his intentions. Looking straight ahead with a flat expression he mumbled on.

"I scared the archbishop's assistant into allowing me to proceed by using my Chicago Family's mob connections. I hooked his self-interest and greed by implying that there would be money in it for him, too. I have not told him my real goal in doing all this praiseworthy stuff of building an orphanage and a church. Very simply I just want to be appointed as an auxiliary bishop within the Archdiocese."

Hearing his own admission of selfish motivations blurting out, Benito experienced a wave of guilt and shame wash over him. He glanced at Sister Florence and saw that she, also, was witnessing his unleashed egotism.

The tense silence of Benito's attack of low self-esteem swelled inside the car filling it with an uncomfortable pressure. Sister Florence rolled down her car window. She breathed in deeply the outside air.

Parking the car in the motel parking lot, they walked through the tropically landscaped courtyard. The swimming pool's blue water sparkled in the soft sunlight. Hearing the giggling of a child they found Mari holding on tightly in a swing as Buck pushed her higher and higher. Buck was excitedly telling her, "You are flying with the birds!" Waving to them, Benito and Florence rested on a near-by bench while Buck and Mari continued their spirited playing. Finished swinging, Buck and Mari ran to join them.

All together they made their way to the motel room to find Mari's mother. Slipping the card key down and up with the click of the lock, Father Benito pushed open the door just as Rosa scrambled from the bed into the bathroom. Fumbling his shirt with one hand, William pushed back his hair with the other, smiling awkwardly as the others walked into the room.
Father Benito and Sister Florence jerked glances at each other. Florence muttered, "Uh oh," under her breath and busied herself with pouring Mari a drink of water. Benito simply sighed, slumping into the easy chair. He muttered under his breath, "We shouldn't be surprised."

During supper at the restaurant, Sister Florence shared that she had contacted a nun friend who was working in the area. Sister Gratia was a member of the Divine Mother Order which ministered in the fields of Community Building and Social Justice. She had invited them to spend the night in the guest quarters of the local college which was staffed by their fellow priests. This generous offer was eagerly accepted and arrangements were made to relocate there. Following supper, they met Sister Gratia who showed the men to one guest house and Sister Florence, Rosa, and Mari, to another. They were able to settle in for a peaceful and proper night's rest.

The next morning Sister Gratia accompanied the group to breakfast in the college's cafeteria. She and Sister Florence sat together at a separate table and had an animated conversation. Sister Gratia shared the details of her social justice work with the homeless, women, minorities, immigrants, gays, elders, and others. The two discussed the problems and best practices that seemed to be of the greatest help. Sister Florence shared about the needs and problems in her work with women and children seeking asylum in Philadelphia. Sister Gratia said that they had strong local allies among their volunteers, Catholic Charities, the college law school staff, as well as their Divine Mother Retreat Center staff. "It is hard work here, but I feel encouraged with what progress we do make. I feel many individuals are helped greatly".

Sister Gratia shared with Sister Florence her personal interest in a special project located in St. Louis, Missouri. "My Order is planning a housing project that intrigues me. I would enjoy offering input into the design to include aspects that foster a sense of community among the residents. I have learned the importance of an individual's need to belong to a community. When that is missing, a person's spirit of worth and determination deteriorate quickly and in many ways." Sister Florence agreed and shared that she had observed the same within her group of asylum-seeking women and children.

The Sisters joined the others for a second cup of coffee. Father Benito reported, "Buck has asked if we could drive him and William back to their parents' home now. And bring Rosa and Mari to their relatives' families." Buck added, "And they might have news of Juan, Diego, Armando, and Gregorio by now! Rosa, won't you be happy to again see your son Diego? And Mari, you will see your big brother!" Rosa's face turned blank. She quickly pasted a stiff smile on it and said, "Yes." She glanced nervously at William who calmly finished drinking his cup of coffee oblivious to her nervousness.

CHAPTER FOURTEEN-JUANS, MOMS, AND SCATTERED PEEPS

July

Father Benito drove. Sister Florence sat next to him. Buck, Rosa with Mari on her lap, and William sat in the back seat. William would occasionally hold hands with Rosa. He made a token effort to hide his affection by nesting their entwined hands between them on the car seat. Father's powerful black Cadillac made good time heading west on the I-10 freeway, speeding along under the vast Texas sky. The car's air conditioner earned everyone's appreciation on this trip. Alternating between the two available radio stations, they listened in turn to cowboys wailing out Waylon's crying songs, then switching to Hispanics weaving hip-hop rhythms into jazzed-up versions of traditional Mexican um-pa.

Rosa was glad for the privacy allowed by the background noise. She wondered to herself what her moves might be when she came face-to-face with her *relatives*. Her worst fear was that Father Benito and Sister Florence would find out that she was a fraud and turn her in at the nearest I.C.E. office. Mari would be taken away from her again. Rosa's throat closed in fear and forced out a muffled scream. Her body shuddered. William felt her distress and put his arm around her shoulders squeezing her tightly against him. Rosa's panic slowly subsided from a full boil to the usual simmering of desperation that she carried within her. She hugged Mari and stroked her baby-fine, oh-so-sweet hair.

Several tortilla and burrito-stops later, they joined the five o'clock traffic on a rural Texas town main street which was twelve blocks long. Recognizing the approaching side street of his family home, Buck pulled himself forward. He leaned his arms on the back of the driver's seat. "Turn right here Father." Passing a row of 1940's bungalow houses, Buck hollered, "Here we are! There's Mom coming out the screen door on the front porch." He waved to her out the window. His Mom eagerly waved back.

They all piled out of the car. Looking around the area they slowly walked through the yard and up the sidewalk onto the front porch. Buck, William, and Mom hugged and hugged each other. Buck introduced his mom, Emma, to everyone. Emma sat down in the porch swing and coaxed Mari to sit on her lap to enjoy a gentle swing. Mari gradually softened and smiled, all the while keeping her gaze fixed upon Rosa and holding onto her Mommy's outstretched hand. Emma beamed and said, "We need some little kids around here. Of course, everyone is invited to my home-cooked supper! Fried okra, Buck! Cornbread, William!" The boys grinned and started into the house. Emma added, "Supper will be ready in thirty minutes. Rosa, would you like to come and help me?" The others scattered, relaxing in the family home and relieved to be in such a pleasant place after the long drive.

Emma made cheerful small talk with Rosa as they bustled around the kitchen. Emma helped Mari sit in the middle of the kitchen floor and pulled out some pots and pans and a large wooden spoon for her to *play cook* supper with them. Emma dropped small bites of raw carrot into Mari's pot and instructed her, "Mari, now cook that, taste it, and tell me if it needs more salt." Mari quickly stirred it and popped it into her mouth and looked up at Emma who laughed and told her, "Good job".

When supper was ready, Emma and Rosa gave Mari two metal pot lids to hold by their wooden knob handles, one in each of her small hands. They led her onto the back porch looking out into the back yard where the others were milling about. Emma helped Mari bang the two lids together creating a clanging and announcing, "Supper is ready!" Walking through the backdoor, Buck and the others filed past Mari chuckling and patting her on the head. Mari gifted them with her bright innocent and happy smiling face.

Following supper Benito and Florence did the dishes. Buck's and William's bedrooms were given to Benito and Florence.

Rosa was given the couch with Mari on a pallet on the floor next to Rosa. William and Buck were assigned the pull-out couch in the den. Buck's Dad was working the night shift. After Mari fell asleep on her "own little bed," William and Rosa sat on the front porch rocking quietly in the swing. The ebb and flow of the chorus of crickets and tree frogs sang under the starlight.

The sunrise welcomed the new day with the early dawn chirps of a robin. It was seconded by the trills of the mocking bird flexing his black and white wings perched in the drought-gnarled elm tree shading the front porch.

Sister Florence, saying her rosary, sat in a rocking chair looking out of her upstairs bedroom window. The sky panorama was powder-puffed with small pink clouds, spotlighted with that unique sunrise touch of pure white. She felt contented with a sense of wonder, gratitude, and a special closeness to The Divine. She addressed The Divine with a wish to" Have me express You today!" Downstairs, she heard the voices of Emma, Buck, and William amid the moving around of pans and dishes in the kitchen. Their occasional laughs of teasing each other mingled pleasantly with the smells of breakfast cooking.

Rosa awoke frightened. She instinctively considered gathering up Mari and sneaking out of the front door. She remembered her mother's desperate face telling her, "Run!" She imagined taking Mari and sneaking through the hedges of the neighborhood yards, hurrying and hiding in the creek bed vegetation, running as fast as she could.

Rosa covered her face with the sheet and tried to block everything out with sleep. Eventually, Mari began waking up and reaching for her. Rosa felt a gladness that Mari was there. She spoke reassuringly to her asking her gently if she were hungry and ready for breakfast? She thought, for right now, at least for this minute, until Mari had eaten breakfast, she would not run. At least, for now…

Father Benito had been up since dawn scribbling drawings for the construction of a new church and an orphanage. He hoped that as he scribbled ideas for how to proceed would flow into his mind. They didn't. He began to wonder what he was to do with Rosa and Mari. He felt uncomfortable about the fake credentials that his Uncle Salvi had scrounged for him.

Now that he was back in his old parish territory, he felt some guilt that he had bailed out of the mess that the parishioners found themselves in after the whites' church had burned down. He had told himself, "It's not your fault. You, too, are burned out. Move on. Get out of this depressing place as fast as you can." He had quickly found himself an upscale job in Washington, D.C. and it came with a very nice salary. He felt he had made savvy choices for himself. He had decided to ignore his guilty feelings and to not live in the past.

There was just one problem. Although he had made a conscious decision to never allow himself to think about it, nor talk about it, he experienced a recurring memory. The occasion of that Sunday morning Mass when out of nowhere that *Abuela* on her knees, uninvited and unwanted, entered into his church designated for the white parishioners. That memory *disturbed his sense of the world's order*. And with it, forever, his peace of mind. With his black ink pen Benito angrily marked big X's blotting out his scribbled drawings. Pushing aside his work, he hurriedly descended downstairs in need of a cup of strong black coffee and a solid breakfast to stabilize his mood.

Following breakfast, Buck excitedly called out, "Come on Rosa! Let's go see your sister-in-law, Elena, and your family across town. Mari! We're going to meet your *Tia!*" He held Mari's hand leading her to the car. Emma called Mari back for a hug good-bye and gave Rosa a hug too. William walked close to Rosa opening the car's back door for her. Settled into Father Benito's Cadillac, they waved goodbye to Emma as they drove slowly through the streets to the other side of town.

William asked Father to drive by the burned down church since he had not yet seen it. Benito hesitated not wanting to be reminded of it but quietly agreed. On the hill, there it was, or was not, over-looking the town. Its blackened foundation and floor were littered with indistinguishable mounds of debris and slivers of charred wood. From the cracks in the concrete steps and floor, sprouting pigweed, tumbleweeds, sunflowers, yucca, and coreopsis (yellow wild flowers) were tentatively reclaiming their ancestral growing grounds.

William wanted to walk the crumbled site. Buck walked it, too, wondering if the wrought-iron votive-candle stand would still be there. It was. Turned upside down with its blackened feet stiff in the air. It was now covered with vines of small blooming wild morning glories known as bindweed. Everyone was silent. Surveying the destruction, they felt as if this were a graveyard. They hesitated to walk there fearing that they might be treading upon sacred relics.

Benito waded through the debris able to make his way to the low step where the communion rail once stood. Standing there facing towards the former main aisle he re-experienced that fateful Sunday when he disgustedly turned away from that *Abuela* who was on her knees before him with her closed eyes and mouth eagerly open. A searing streak of sadness and remorse travelled through him like a streak of lightening. He sank to his knees and began to sob. He did not know what was happening to him but he could not stop it. In his mind's eye he saw the *Abuela* experiencing in the core of her heart the shudder of grief and shame at being rejected by her Lord in Holy Communion. A flood of realization washed over him that it was *he* who had committed the murder of her hope of being loved dearly by her Christ.

Decimated, he continued to sob, wilted by his remorse and shame in this devastated place of worship. Slowly returning to the present, he sighed deeply and looked up. Sister Florence was quietly sitting beside him. She gently placed her hand on his shoulder and waited. They finally arose and slowly returned to the car.

Walking the perimeter of the foundation using his tape measure, William periodically stopped, removed a small spiral notepad and pen from his shirt pocket, and wrote down the feet and inches of the dimensions. When they returned to the car,

Buck asked, "Father, let's stop at the other church, the one for the Hispanics. I want to show it to Rosa and Mari. Okay?" Benito quietly agreed but again reluctant to revisit this part of his past.

The small adobe structure looked like it had remained the same for a thousand years. Squatting among several spreading brushy mesquite trees, the primitive church looked lonely and as if it had been abandoned by some long-ago native tribe. Father pushed open the never-locked front door. Walking inside, their eyes gradually accustomed themselves to the dim light. The thick walls kept the air cool. Patches of flaking paint splotched the ceiling and walls. There were sparse furnishings and the atmosphere spoke of poverty.

To the left side of the main altar, on a minor shelf, stood a three-foot-high stone statue of Our Lady of Guadalupe clasping her hands in eternal prayer, dressed in a faded blue painted dress. A long-stemmed dried pink rose lay on the kneeling rail before her. Father surveyed the place with the same impatience he had felt when had hurriedly said Mass here previously, always glad to leave. He sat down in the back pew wondering how it was that he had ever ended up here. And now here he was again.

Rosa and Mari explored the aisles and pews. Rosa felt a sense of comfort and familiarity from this type of church. She felt drawn to the statue and kneeled down to pray there. She instinctively fingered the stone hem of the dress of Our Lady. Her fingers slipped into small indentations and grooves worn there by countless others who had come here before her for refuge. Finding no words in her mind, she squeezed the hem harder and harder realizing that she was holding on to it for dear life. Bowing her head, she cried softly turning all her insurmountable griefs, problems, and needs over to Our Lady for solving.

In her mind, Rosa saw images of her mother smiling at her. Then images of her grandmother and the faces of many other mothers, smiling in support and love at their little girls. Those girls were holding their little girl dolls, cooing and comforting them. Rosa sensed the presences of many mothers and young girls radiating out in long lines back into time and forward into the future. Rosa felt included in the destiny of the chain of life-supportive mothering. A sense of encouragement calmed her feelings of desperation. She began to feel immersed within a pinkish dew of hope. Rosa looked up into the face of Our Lady and with a slight smile whispered, "Thank you."

Father Benito watched Rosa while Mari played on the floor at her feet. He was mesmerized with seeing her experience praying to Our Lady of Guadalupe and marveled at her changed demeanor. He wondered what had happened seeing a new aura of peace come over her. He thought, "That is the way Sister Florence is. How do they have that?" He thought, "I'll never understand these women."

Back in the car, the group drove through the dusty and narrow dirt streets in the other part of town. Buck directed Father until they arrived at Juan's family home. Juan's mother, Elena, came suspiciously out of the small house onto the front porch. With a mixture of fear and aggressiveness, she inspected the car and its occupants as it stopped in the street. Buck grinned at her and waved as he opened his car door and approached her. Recognizing him, Elena greeted him with respect and rather formally. Buck wanted them to hug but returned her respectful and formal greeting. He introduced everyone to each other except Rosa and Mari. Elena slightly bowed to Father Benito and Sister Florence keeping her eyes looking at the ground. She was quiet and waited for Father to speak.

Buck eagerly reached out taking hold of Rosa's hand. He pulled her from behind the others presenting her and Mari to Elena. With a big smile he addressed Elena announcing, "Elena, look who we found and brought home to you!! Your sister, Rosa! Diego's Mom! And his little sister, Mari, your little niece!" Buck grinned and giggled looking back and forth between Elena and Rosa waiting for their delighted responses. Elena looked at Rosa with a blank expression which matched Rosa's expression. As Elena began to step back and turn away,

92

Rosa stepped in front of Elena, fell on her knees, picked up the hem of Elena's skirt and held it to her mouth, kissing it. Rosa kept her eyes to the ground waiting for Elena's response.

Elena knew what this meant. She hesitated. Looked at the priest, the nun, Buck, and his big brother, all white people. Legal U.S. citizens in a big black car. Then she looked at the child who was beginning to softly cry and at this kneeling Hispanic woman frozen in fear, begging at her feet.

Letting out a deep sigh, Elena gently bent down and touched Rosa's arms helping her stand up. Extending a hand to the child, Elena motioned to Mari and pulled her up against her apron-covered leg. Elena, keeping her eyes to the ground, turned and spoke humbly to the priest, "Thank you for uniting our family. We are grateful." Elena gently herded Rosa and Mari in front of her onto the porch and safely into the house. Elena closed the door behind the three of them leaving the whites free to drive away with no further obligation.

Looking out of the front room window from behind the white laced curtains, Rosa watched William being driven away. Out of the car's rear window he sadly peered back at her.

CHAPTER FIFTEEN-BORDER'S BY-WAYS

July

Father drove slowly back through the town's pot-holed streets. He felt dejected. The car seemed empty. William felt the same way. Sister observed, "We're going to miss them. I wish that the transfer had felt like a happier one." They were now driving down Main Street. Buck waved out the window and yelled, "Hi, Cody!" to one of his friends who was riding by on his bike. Father pulled up to a gas station with a cafe attached to it. William volunteered, "I'll get the pump, Father." Father turned to Sister Florence. "Sister, let's go have a bite. Okay?" She followed him into the café and they sat in a booth overlooking the parking lot. Buck called out, "Go on without me! I'll come home later." and ran down the sidewalk to catch up with Cody. They saw Buck overtake Cody on his bike. Cody stopped long enough to let Buck hop up to sit on the handlebars, all arms and legs poking and bent like a grasshopper. They peddled speeding down the street.

William joined Benito and Florence in the booth but soon excused himself as a friend was motioning to him to come to sit with him in another booth. William reconnected with his friend Brian. Brian had put together a construction crew and invited William to work for him. William took him up on his offer. Their visit would lead to Brian honking at William's curb at six o'clock the next morning. He offered William his extra tool belt as William climbed into Brian's "tuff" red F-350 pickup truck. William felt eager to build something.

Sitting in the booth, Father Benito felt distracted and eventually said to Sister Florence, "I don't really know what I am doing here. I feel out of place, you know?" She nodded, yes. Continuing, he shared, "I ought to be wanting to put together the project of building a church and an orphanage, muscling my way up towards clinching a bishop's rank but …." His voice trailed off as his gaze wandered out the window.

He felt that he had nothing to say. He watched the people filling their pickups with gas. His mind felt empty. Looking at the people sitting in the other booths he noticed a small elderly woman eating alone. He wondered if he knew her. She was withdrawn with a flat unhappy expression on her pale white face and in her dull blue eyes. She was concentrating on negotiating her hamburger meal, taking slow careful bites without much interest in the food. Benito thought, "She looks like how I feel."

He realized that he did recognize her. She was Woodrow's wife Irene, from his former parish. He remembered how animated she had been that Sunday when she had defiantly stood up and ordered him in a loud, stern voice, "You had better not!" Then, he remembered himself doing as she wished. He had coldly turned away from the *Abuela* refusing to administer to her the Bread of Life.

Again, the scene passively played out before his mind's eye like it wasn't really him that had been there. He was left feeling even more dejected. He felt detached, not really caring about any of them. Saying to Sister Florence as he stood up, "Let's get out of here, okay?" Observing his irritation, she nodded, yes. William motioned them to move on without him indicating that he was staying with his buddy, Brian. They left, driving out of the parking lot as slowly as they had driven in. Benito thought, "Everything around here creeps at its own *petty pace*." He smiled to himself remembering Shakespeare.

By the time their car creeped back and parked at Buck's home, they could see down the street that Buck and Cody were flying on the bike towards them. With Buck barely balancing himself hanging onto the handle bars, they swerved and swayed up to the front bumper of Benito's dusty black Cadillac. Jumping off, Buck excitedly said to Father Benito, "You've got to come with us back to talk to Rosa and Elena! They have heard news about Juan! Follow me, Father!" For this trip Buck jumped on his own bike. Dodging potholes in the streets they arrived at Elena's home. She and Rosa, with Mari on her lap, were sitting

95

on the front porch on an old backbench car seat. Elena offered each of the guests a battered folding metal chair.

Seated and settled down, Elena explained that a neighbor who had returned from a trip to the border near the town of Eagle Pass, Texas and Piedras Negras, Mexico, reported that he had heard that Elena's nephews Juan, Diego, Armando, and Gregorio were wandering north along the border following Highway 2 on the Mexican side. They were in hiding making their way up the Rio Grande River looking for a safe crossing opportunity. They had joined a group of traveling illegal immigrants. Elena was obviously nervous and feeling distressed yet relieved to have any news of them. Rosa was alert to Elena's story and feelings trying to respond in kind.

Keeping her eyes cast downward, Elena turned to Father Benito. In a humble but insistent tone she asked him, "Father, you will go find them in your large official car? You will bring them home to our family? *Si, Senor Father? Por va for. Si, Padre Benito? Si?"* Elena, eyes still downcast held herself very still intensely facing Benito. She was indicating that she intended to not move an inch until the Reverend Father agreed.

Father Benito squirmed in his hard metal chair. He felt very uncomfortable. He quickly stood up, rubbing his bottom with his hands. Making his way towards the driver's door of his car he fumbled the keys out of his pocket. Finding the ignition key, he positioned it between his fingers ready to use. Sister Florence swiftly glided, as usual, faster than Buck believed any person could move, into the front passenger seat of the car. She was prepared for Benito as he slipped into his driver's seat and pushed his key into the ignition. With her hand Sister Florence covered his hand, holding it tightly. Staring at the center of the steering wheel, Benito's mind flashed the thought, "This must be déjà vu." Turning to each other another intense discussion began.

Watching them Buck turned to Elena to explain, "When they do this it can take a while." She relaxed saying, *"Claro."* Observing Benito and Florence sitting in the car animatedly

96

gesturing Buck and Rosa exchanged knowing glances. Mischievously, Rosa assumed an exaggerated look of pious devotion. Looking up at the sky with hands clasped she fell to her knees. Buck laughed. Breaking character, Rosa laughed too. Presently, Buck asked Elena if she had cooked any of her tasty tamales lately. He was getting hungry. She smiled and proceeded into the kitchen motioning to Rosa. Buck could soon hear sounds coming from the kitchen of Mari helping play-cook tamales.

The discussion in the car finally drew to a close, summed up with a period of silent prayer. By this time Buck and company had enjoyed most of Elena's delicious tamales. Back again, sitting on their hard metal chairs, Benito and Florence were quiet. They gratefully ate Elena's offered homemade treat enjoying the hot spicy smells and tastes. The others respected their silence watching them in patient expectation.

His meal concluded, Father Benito announced in a flat serious tone, "I will drive to Piedras Niegras and search for the boys. God willing." Taking a deep breath, he mockingly looked up addressing the sky, "And Sister Florence willing!" Everyone laughed in relief.

CHAPTER SIXTEEN-BORDER BOUND

July

Early eastern sunrays slanted low through the driver's side windows of the sleek black Cadillac caressing the sleepy seekers lulled by the humming highway. Benito felt that the only thing that he knew for sure in this mission was that he had said, *Yes.* Other than that, he had no assurances of what was happening.

He wondered what advice his aged seminary teachers would have given him for this situation. Old Gaetti would frown and shake his head *No, no.* as he always said *No* to anything that wasn't in some rubric book somewhere. Old Giovani would just laugh at him, and say, "I wish that I were younger and were there, too! How is the tequila? Is there really a worm in the bottle of the bottle?" When it came down to making real life decisions, those guys were never of much help.

He glanced at Sister Florence sitting next to him, her sleepy head bobbing slightly. He reflected, *I wouldn't even be here if it weren't for her. Who is she, really, and why is she in my life at all?* He had no answers. To anything.

Sister Florence had decided that she wanted her friend, Sister Gratia, to accompany them to the border because of Gratia's immigration connections and experience with border circumstances in this part of Texas. Gratia had agreed and had arrived the following day accompanied by her self-appointed escort and protector, Hans. Military trained, a big and burley blue-eyed Nordic blond warrior, had her back. Glancing in the rearview mirror, Benito eyed Han's hummer which he knew was stocked to the gills with survival gear. Hans was driving it with expert skill just as he handled everything that he touched. Benito judged Hans to be the most competent man he had yet met. Alert to his surroundings at all times, he chauffeured Gratia, dedicated to "keeping her safe." He agreed that Buck would ride along in the back seat.

Several hours later, stopping in Eagle Pass at the border

between the U.S. and Mexico on the Rio Grande River, they gassed up their vehicles not knowing when they would come upon the next opportunity. Gathering in the shade at the gas pump, they discussed what was next. Sister Gratia suggested that they inquire about the whereabouts of Juan and his immigrant group at the informal camp of traditional Kickapoo Native Americans, illegals, and homeless people who gathered under the old Eagle Pass International Bridge Number 1. It was located adjacent to the new bridge, Number 2. Agreeing, they safely parked Benito's car placing it under the paid care of an employee of the gas station and piled into Hans' tank.

Driving through the weeds west of the bridge near Shelby Park and down Rio Road, Hans slowly wound along following the sandy path to the river bank. Seeing no one, they exited the car and casually relaxed under the bridge spanning above them. In silence they watched the dark green murky water flow over its wide expanse of riverbed. The fastmoving current split through several long brush-covered islands and sand bars. The powerful river was interweaving deep channels with its turbulent waters, warning off anyone attempting to cross here.

Presently people began to appear, coming out of hiding and going about their business and keeping their distance from these strangers. Hans observing it all causally, walked near a small sun-browned man. Hans humbly stated that they were searching for some friends that they had heard were hiding and traveling this way looking for a safe crossing. The man listened kindly stating that he and his Kickapoo Indian relatives had lived under this bridge for many years. The Tribe recently had been granted a small piece of land about thirteen miles down-river southeast of town at Rosita South. Most of his family lived in government housing there. The Tribe had a medical clinic a casino and a school. However, he still preferred to live here in their traditional camp area. Abruptly, he moved away into the brush. Not at all surprised, Hans sat down to patiently wait.

Eventually, the man named, Harjo, re-appeared presenting his nephew, Juan, who seemed to be about fifteen years old.

Harjo offered to Hans, "Juan has agreed to guide you along the river. Our people know it well." Pausing for several minutes while they both listened to the slushing of the river among the cattails, Harjo continued. "His mother's house needs an air conditioner and a refrigerator." Following a brief hesitation, he quickly looked at Hans directly in the eye, and added. "And a TV. The broken ones are on the front porch. They don't work." Harjo became silent, restlessly waiting for Hans to respond. Hans reached into his pocket for his wallet and handed over some cash saying, "Thanks, Harjo." Smiling, Harjo slipped away as he had arrived, disappearing into the brush.

Hans and Juan looked each other over without seeming to notice each other, their eyes never meeting. Hans said, "Good. Come with me." They joined the others, squeezed into the car, and churned sand under the tires on their way up and out of the river bottom. Reentering the highway leading over the bridge, they passed through the Mexican checkpoint without a problem.

Juan, sitting in the back seat directly behind Hans, pointed him to turn left to travel south on Mexico Highway 5, then east-southeast on Highway 2 towards Laredo. The highway followed the river downstream. Juan occasionally tapped Hans on the shoulder motioning him to pull over into off-road and unofficial rest-stops surrounded by mesquite underbrush close to the river bank. Juan would exit the car, hurrying into the thick brush, then soon return, motioning that they were to continue driving.

This routine continued until nightfall. Juan said, "It is time to camp and sleep until the sun comes up." So, they did. Hans put the boys to work setting up the tents that he had stowed. He cooked supper over a small campfire which created no smoke that could be detected by a possible foe, anywhere out there. Thanks to Hans' competence, they all had a fairly comfortable night's sleep.

Buck arose about an hour before daylight. He walked quietly in the sand down to the river, hearing its purr calling in the darkness telling him when he had come to the water's edge. Sitting down leaning back on his two stiffened arms and elbows, he tilted his head backwards to see the starry sky. He muffled a gasp at the clearness of the desert air magnifying the morning star, Venus.

The panorama of sparkling stars, their height or depth spreading back away into who-knows-how-far, seared overwhelming-beauty into his soul. Tears involuntarily brimmed his eyes. Mesmerized as if watching a movie, he experienced the simultaneous lightening of the sky and the fading away of each of the stars.

They faded one at a time, bowing off-stage to the next act. The purpling, pinking, oranging and white-tinging streaks of sunrise painted everything in sight. As the sun slowly peeked up and over the horizon, Buck felt like clapping at the wondrous performance. He felt happy and so lucky. Yes, he was *Lucky Bucky*, as some of his friends fondly called him.

Hans cooked plenty of breakfast for everyone and served each of them with a friendly smile. Smells of campfire cooking bacon and boiling coffee softened everyone's mood and energized them to take up the hunt once more.

Juan's and Han's routine of stopping, searching and starting, resumed as they traveled farther down the river. As they neared the junction of Highway 85 and Highway 70, which led south into the interior of the State of Nuevo Leon and the city of Monterey, Juan became more alert.

Hans suspected that Juan was sensing that they were closing in on their prey. That he was. At the next stop, Juan practically ran down to the river. Time passed. About thirty minutes later, here they all came. A skittish bunch sneaking up the river bank. Buck jumped out of the car calling, "Juan, Juan! We found you! Diego! Gregorio! Armando!" They all hugged. Buck began to sniffle. One by one, they sniffled all around as a rush of relief flooded among them. Juan related that most of the illegal immigrants that had been in their group decided to try to cross the river border downstream near Laredo. Juan and his group decided to travel upriver towards Piedras Negras to cross the river.

The realization began to affect the boys as to how tough their travels had been. The rush of relief weakened their knees. Soon all were sitting down, resting. Observing what was happening, Hans rummaged among his supplies and handed out chocolate bars and sodas. Smiles and chuckles gradually began to bubble up.

Eventually, Hans indicated that it was time to "get going." Counting heads Hans calculated that transporting them all would be possible with a bit of reconfiguration. He popped open his self-inflating raft and fastened it upon the outside roof of the car. Four immigrants crawled onto it, laying themselves side by side, alternating head to toe. Hans covered them with a secured tarp. The others squeezed into the seats and hatch area and off they drove retracing their route back up the river towards Piedras Niegras.

Approaching the far southern outskirts of Piedras Negras, Kickapoo Juan tapped Hans on the shoulder and motioned for him to pull off the road into a hidden clearing on the river bank. "Unload the immigrants here." he told Hans. Having done so everyone gathered around Kickapoo Juan who motioned them to hunker down into the position of sitting on their heels in a circle. Touching his ears and looking at each of them, they all began to listen intently. The birds soon grew accustomed to their presence and resumed their usual chirruping. Juan puckered his lips and let out a long slow and low-pitched whistle that vibrated into a musical sentence. Silent again, he whispered, "Whistling. Old traditional Kickapoo talk." Finger to his lips, they continued listening for a response.

Sounding from far across the river a low faint whistle drifted into their circle. Juan smiled. The worried faces changed into hopeful grins as they exchanged glances with each other. They shifted into more relaxed postures. Juan returned the whistle, this time with a slightly higher pitch. Waiting quietly, another faint whistle was heard this time from much closer. The group grinned again. Juan then gave a different response. He broke his whistle into eleven chirps. Whispering, he said in English, "They

102

wanted to know how many of us."

Listening again, they were startled by Sister Florence's abrupt squeal. Showing themselves, three young Kickapoo men stepped into the clearing, alertly observing the group. Juan stood. Using Kickapoo word language, he conversed in a friendly tone with Lawrence Wahpepaw, his friend. Presently, Kickapoo Juan asked Father Benito how many needed to cross the river? Benito turned to the others and they began a serious discussion about who wanted to go with these young men to try to cross the river.

The sun was beginning to set. Hans looked at the sky, the camp clearing, and the river perimeter. He announced that they would be setting up camp for the night. He directed Buck and the others to set up the tents, a cooking area, and a latrine lean-to. They began to settle in and soon Hans and others had combined their food items and concocted a tasty meal that they were all gratefully eating, including their Kickapoo guides.

In the deep twilight, Buck walked down to tell the river goodnight. Standing on the bank, he observed the abundance of cattails in this area. Surprised, he noticed Kickapoo Juan sitting unnoticed, also watching the river. Juan was occasionally throwing bits of broken cattail stalks into various sections of the river. Buck watched intently. Juan spoke in English quietly, "The currents." Buck noticed anew the floating stalks. Some moved swiftly downstream. Others were almost stationary. Others were washed into piles against unseen sand bars. "That is how we know where it is safe to cross." They shared in silence the privacy of the river's open space. Together they listened to the music of the trickling water. They saw the rising moon's light breaking into shards sparkling on the surface of the dark water. Looking at each other in the near blackness of the night, they smiled and returned up the sandy bank to the campsite.

Sharing a tent, the Juan's began to have a heart-to-heart talk. Kickapoo Juan told Hispanic Juan that he felt that they were *brothers in the Native way*. He explained, "Like me, you have a heritage of Native American. Your ancestors were Tribal

103

members living in Central America when they intermarried with the Spanish, and others, from Europe. Therefore, you, like me, probably have the *second sight* ability." Continuing he elaborated, "We have the ability to see the world around us from an "interrelated" viewpoint that whites frequently can't see. We naturally can sense the connections among ourselves and all the animals, plants, air, water, fire, and earth. Almost every Tribe has language for this *second sight*. The Sioux use: *na tak ee ah see*. The Potawatomi use: *nden we' mag nek*. These are roughly translated into the English as: All Our Relations.

When we enter into a trance of that state of knowing, we find that it is a *current* with great power. My Elders have taught me, and I can train you, in learning to use that power. Most whites don't understand anything about this *current*. If they come across us using it, they call it superstition and leave us alone. That is a good thing, we think. If they were to learn how to use it, they would undoubtedly use it for their greed.

"Have you ever wondered what our role is among all the other created things? About how we, our human species, fit into the food chain? About what our unique contribution abilities are to the rest of *all our relations*?

"Many whites believe that their goal in life is to be as greedy as possible. To gather the "most" stuff for themselves, alone. And to pee on everything they can in order to mark it as "belonging" to them. And then if they can't have something, they try to destroy it to prevent anyone else from having it.

"We Natives, using our *second sight,* don't see the world from that viewpoint, do we, Juan? Do you?"

Juan had never heard anyone ever describe this type of thinking before. He was listening intently and thinking hard. What he was hearing seemed to fit him like a hand inside a glove.

He responded, "Exactly! I see how everything can be shared. How there is enough for everyone to be okay. And that makes me feel so *different* from whites.

"And angry at them when they keep my people from having

what is really needed to survive and be happy. Simple things, like food, clothing, and shelter, and being able to live together safely as a family." Juan began to tear up as he thought about his own *Abuelita*, now dead, and his relatives who were in immigrant detention centers or running and hiding.

Kickapoo Juan comforted him and asked him, "My Native brother, what is it that *you want?* Think about it. Then after this trip is over come back and find me. Maybe, together, we can do what it is that you are needing to do. We will be 'Juan 'N Juan,' okay?" Feeling comfort in their shared feelings of connection, they soon fell asleep.

Hans had built a very small campfire of driftwood and twigs for "his girls." The women had gathered to sleep in their own area, with Hans on watch nearby. They were sitting on their serapes and blankets, circling their hearth, absorbing human comfort from each other's presence.

They shared their personal stories, drinking hot *yerbe'mate'* tea. Their stories were filled with sufferings, tragic separations, abuse, terror, traumas, hopes, longings, and sometimes, love. Under the protective arm of the privacy of darkness, they shared their stories. Hiding within their cloaks of fear, some cried, some were numb, some were angry, while others were simply exhausted to the bone, speaking so softly that they were barely audible.

Sister Florence and Sister Gratia sitting next to each other, listened with deep compassion. They knew that they were simultaneously praying for the woman who was telling her story and suffering so deeply.

One by one, the women, some leaning against each other, drifted off to sleep, hoping to enter the world of blessed peace and rest. Each and every one, first, hoped for the safety of their precious loved ones, on this night, scattered wherever they might be.

Yet awake were the Sisters and Josie. Staring at the fire, Josie spoke softly, "I am thinking that Our Lady of Guadalupe wants me to tell you about her wish." Alert, the Sisters asked her to continue. Josie recounted the story told to her by her mother and grandmother. About the donkey and Our Lady's wishes to build a church and to free the souls of those trapped on the mountain plateau. The Sisters listened with interest.

Josie said, "We went there, built the church, but Our Lady said there was more to do about helping the trapped souls. Maybe, you and Father Benito are supposed to go there to help them?" Josie finished and continued staring at the fire lost in thought. The Sisters looked at each considering. Josie stretched out and fell asleep. The Sisters retired to the tent that Hans had protectively provided for them and surrendered to deep sleep.

The birds' early crescendo of sounds swelled, as the sun rose above the willows and a huge cottonwood tree which shaded the campsite. Relaxed, with feelings of a fresh infusion of some relief at being rescued, the group slowly roused. Milling around and eating their stand-up breakfasts, they completed their planning of who was going with the Kickapoos to venture through the watery border to the other side.

Buck and Miguel said that they wished to go with the Kickapoo guides. Hans agreed that on his return he would pick them up at the Kickapoo reservation. The immigrants who were hesitating shared hesitant glances with each other, then, hurried after the Native guides who were their best hope in light of desperate circumstances. Watching them stumble through the brush and sand, the nuns, priest, Hans, Juan, Diego, Gregorio, Armando, and Josie waved good-bye with as much encouragement as they could put into their waving arms.

Hans and the boys efficiently broke camp and compactly loaded up the gear, ready for what would come next. Sitting on stumps around the smoldering campfire, the others were discussing their situation. The Sisters conversed with Josie about her willingness to lead them back to La Place de las Animas. She agreed in order to obey the wishes of Our Lady of Guadalupe.

Now, they needed to ask Father Benito what he thought about helping to rescue the trapped souls. Sister Florence inwardly chuckled considering his probable reaction of flight.

106

She causally rolled up the long sleeves of her habit and looked his way. Walking past Hans, who was resting in the shade of the cottonwood tree, she said to him privately, "Don't let Father Benito get to your car keys." Hans replied, "Yes, Sister" without knowing what she was talking about.

Sister Florence took her time walking across the camp site towards Benito. He noticed the slow deliberation of her approach and wondered if he should be worried. Sister Florence was thinking, praying, fingering the rosary beads hanging from her waist belt. She occasionally lifted her eyes heavenward as her lips silently moved. Watching her actions, Benito moved his position to hide himself behind the cottonwood tree out of her sight.

He heard the crackling of the leaves and twigs from her footsteps. They halted on the opposite side of the tree trunk. He waited apprehensively listening. Her soft voice spoke to him, "Father Benito? I need to ask you something." Benito knew that tone. He remained silent. He wanted to run. He looked around to find the location of the car.

She spoke again, "Father Benito? Let's go for a walk along the river. I need to ask you something. Okay?" Her gentleness was so inviting that he found himself *wanting* to fall for her old trick of talking him into doing very distasteful things. He was silent. He felt miserable, and happy, both at the same time. Once more, she murmured, "Father Benito? Come with me. Please?" She slowly began walking towards the river. He paused in relief that she had walked away. Then, he couldn't help himself. He hurried after her.

Next to her Father Benito assumed a pace matching her slow walking and waited for the bad news of her request. It came. "Father, Rosa has told us that, according to her mother's grandmother's accounts, as well as her own recollections, Our Lady of Guadalupe told them that she wanted us to help rescue the many souls who are trapped on the top of a plateau in Mexico. We are asking you to help us. Will you take us there and help rescue them, please?"

Benito couldn't believe this implausible request. He wondered if Florence were joking. He stopped walking and looked at her in astonishment. She was serious and was looking back at him expectantly. Exasperated, he blurted out, "Florence, how can you ask me to do this! I don't even believe in all that superstitious stuff! No one in their right mind would go on such a mission!" He continued with righteous indignation: "Why, I'm an educated man. I graduated from the top seminary. In Rome! At the Vatican! That type of superstition is banned from all the Rubric books which have the stamps of the Imprimatur of the Holy See. I am not a heretic!"

And he continued with his ranting. Sister Florence countered his objections with multiple arguments.

She added that Sister Gratia wanted to go to honor Our Lady of Guadalupe as well because she belonged to the nuns' Order of Divine Mother who were dedicated to the Blessed Mother Mary. On and on, the heated exchange flared between them with their arms flinging up and down for emphasis.

The others were comfortably lounging in the shade at the camp site watching them spar verbally. Buck explained, "This may take a while. I've seen it before. Hans, how about some sodas to drink?" Hans agreed, and the group watched the priest and nun flinging their arms around in the air making their points, raising and lowering their voices, with Sister Florence occasionally crying. It, indeed, did "take a while."

Eventually, they walked back in silence, both obviously praying. After a period of silence, Benito announced in a matter-of-fact tone, "We'll be travelling to a plateau in Mexico where there are trapped souls. We'll rescue them. God willing. And, (sliding a glance at her) Sister Florence willing. Hans, will you please drive us there?" Hans, in his good-soldier's obedient voice, answered, "Yes Sir, Father!"

FATHER BENITO'S WILDERNESS

They all piled into the hummer and headed back down Mexico's Highway 2, turning onto Highway 85 towards Monterrey, on their way to La Place de las Animas, the place of ghosts. As the miles bumped and swayed along, Father Benito reflected on his situation. He wondered what were the real reasons that he was driving into the mountain wilderness. What was happening to him that he was feeling so disillusioned about his career within the church? Why could he not dismiss that past incident of excluding that old *abuela* from the whites' parish. That type of racism was usual in most places. It was taken for granted and it never bothered him, or any of the white parishioners, or their priests, or bishops, before. Why was he being pulled into this superstition involving Our Lady of Guadalupe? He felt that he was becoming too personally involved with all these immigrants and their problems. And with these nuns! He wished that everything in his life would go back to being normal. He wanted to stop this pilgrimage, turn around, get all of these people out of his personal life, and return to his comfortable apartment in Washington, D.C. His life seemed out of control. He felt a small fear beginning to grow in the pit of his stomach. What was going to happen to him? High in the distant sky ahead, he noticed a flock of black buzzards slowly circling. Ominously, the mountains loomed ahead.

CHAPTER SEVENTEEN-GHOST PLATEAU

July

Exiting south on Highway 85 several hours later, they arrived in Monterrey. They refueled the hummer, then themselves, with dinner at a café. Hans purchased more supplies and a detailed map of the local mountain area. He, Benito, and Josie examined the map closely locating the general area of the plateau. Josie explained to them that its exact location could only be found by those drawn to it through their sins. Hearing this, Benito flinched in silent unbelief, thinking, "These superstitious people! I am on a fool's mission here."

Hans noticed that "his girls" were wearing down. He announced that the group would be spending the night in a motel with showers and real beds. The women smiled gratefully at him. Hans beamed at their appreciation. Upon check-in, he arranged for laundry service and a maid to supply them with whatever "woman things" they needed. Hans wanted the best for "his girls."

Following a hearty breakfast of *ranchos huevos,* they proceeded driving up and down, winding back into the mountains. Coming upon a small village with a single store, they stopped and inquired about the area beyond where this road turned into a foot path. The owner replied, "Only donkeys can travel there. Do you wish to rent my donkeys? *Si, no problemo,* you rent my donkeys? Cheap."

Hans wanted to find another approach by which he could drive his hummer to the destination.

Juan confidently volunteered that he could easily lead some of them along the donkey path to the plateau. He guessed that it might take them about an hour to reach the plateau. Hans stated that he definitely wanted to stay with his hummer. He pointed out that he could drive the longer route and estimated that he could arrive at the plateau in about six hours. Everyone grew quiet personally considering which route to take.

Juan spoke, "Diego, Armando and Gregorio, come with me,

and you. too, Father Benito. And Sister Florence." He looked at them expectantly. Hans spoke, "Sister Gratia come with me. And you, too, Josie. You can show us the way." He looked at them expectantly. No one offered any alternative suggestions, so they all agreed to the proposed plans. Hans and company quickly entered the car and departed down the mountain road.

Juan led his team to the trail head. They surveyed the rocky narrow path winding along the mountain side. Father Benito hesitated when seeing the challenging terrain. He hurried back into the store. Soon he returned walking from the back corral leading two donkeys. One was heaped with camping provisions and the other with a saddle that seemed awkwardly oversized for the sturdy little animal. Joining the group, he noticed their surprised and dismayed reactions.

He became aware of the humor in their unlikely situation. He performed an elaborate bow before Sister Florence, presenting "A mule for Sister Sara." She smiled uncertainly and let Benito help her aboard the humble creature. Benito motioned to Juan and the boys to proceed. Following, he gallantly led the dutiful donkeys carrying Sister Sara over the rocky trail. Sister Sara fingered her rosary beads and marveled at the magnificent mountains.

Speculating, she asked Father Benito, who was walking beside her, "Benito, how are you planning to rescue the trapped souls?" Caught by surprise it occurred to him that he had no idea since he thought the whole idea was an imaginary superstition. "Well, Sister Sara, do you really think that this whole scenario of 'trapped souls' even exists?" he inquired with an elitist sense of humor. Florence was quiet. She said, "You might be surprised, Benito. What would you do if it were a real situation and the souls needed your help? What did your seminary training teach you about that realm of that possibility?"

Benito realized how serious this was to Florence. Soberly he thought aloud, "There is a Catholic tradition of purgatory, as you are aware. This situation might be related to that doctrine. That is, if 'the situation' even exists. And a St. Paul epistle contains the exhortation, 'It is a holy and wholesome thought to pray for the dead.' Then, of course, most of the information about purgatory, heaven, hell, and the devil, that has become common myth, originates with Dante's fictitious novels from the middle ages in Europe. Another Catholic tradition is exorcism. However, the situation of 'trapped souls on the top of a plateau' does not appear to fall into this category of needing an exorcism from a type of possession by a devil, although it might be related in a way that we currently do not know.

"From the perspective of science and critical thinking certain questions need to be explored: what happened to the souls that correlates to them being trapped? What concomitant interventions need to occur to free the trapped souls? And, of course, there is the human condition of being immersed in a material world (incarnation), while simultaneously being under the influence of a spirit world (having a soul). This presents the problem of how to negotiate the interaction between the two worlds which is considered to be one of the universal mysteries of humanity."

Benito thoughtfully concluded his analysis in answer to Florence's question. He waited for her response.

Concerned, she offered, "Father, your mission to free these trapped souls is extremely important to many on this side and on the other side. We will keep a vigil of continuous prayer and support for you while you are on this mission. Hold in your mind that Sister Gratia and I will be here spiritually holding onto you. *You could be entering a realm of great risk. Your life and soul could be in serious danger."* Sister Florence's grave tone of warning disturbed Benito.

He stopped walking and sat down on a nearby rock. Upset, his forehead sweating, he watched the mules continue on ahead, their small hooves delicately stepping through the loose gravel, swaying the nun back and forth in the large saddle.

Benito needed some time to think. If Florence considered this situation to be real and serious, maybe, he needed to reevaluate what he was doing on this extended camping trip.

112

Although, while in the seminary he had studied the early church martyrs, he never considered that he himself might ever be exposed to such a possibility. He had planned to always have a desk type of job with no danger to his life involved. Being a parish priest, and within his current immigration related employment, he seemed safe enough.

It was beginning to occur to Benito that his was an intellectual and bureaucratic form of religious belief. He could argue theological questions as well as the next priest. He could quickly discern when ignorant congregants were blindly following emotional and faith-based superstitions, rather than the official doctrines issued by approved clerical authorities.

His general career plan included developing administrative skills, especially, money management and development/fund raising. Some church clergy dealt with million-dollar budgets. The social status ladder of hierarchy was climbed on rungs of upward steps of fiscal responsibilities. These required advanced skills of political networking and manipulation. And one's conscience had to be trained to flexibly use aggressive instincts of gaining power and control of capital and financial assets.

He recognized that his mob Family valued these same achievements. He had naturally accepted that his Family would consider it only normal that his personal success in the church would depend upon leveraging and muscling his way up into the position of a bishop. They expected it as a reflection upon the status of their Family. Perhaps, to the point of demanding it of him. And Uncle Salvi fully intended for their Family to make sure that Benito would be "successful." It was not a matter of what Benito personally wanted after all. Benito asked himself, *"I'm just following the normal course of doing what all priests do in the organization, right?"* But, now, for the first time he wasn't sure the answer was, yes!

He resumed walking on the path. Ahead, the others had moved into a shady clearing, resting and waiting for him to catch up. Respectfully, they did not question him but looked at him for further instructions. He motioned for Juan to proceed. Rounding

113

an outcrop of overhanging rock, Juan called back, "I see it. La Place de las Animas. It's covered in a bluish haze, like before." He hesitated a bit over-long. Benito guessed that he might be feeling skittish about going closer. Moving up in front of Juan, Benito said, "So, that's it, eh? Let's go free the trapped souls, *amigos*." grinning. That cheered up the boys. They resumed hiking forward.

With enthusiasm, Sister Florence floated the question, "Does anyone see the chapel?" Diego assisted her down from the large saddle. The two of them began exploring with Diego leading and reflecting, "I remember the water pool being in this direction. The chapel was next to it." Curving into a stone walled enclosure, they arrived. The pool was reflecting sun sparkles on its clear calm surface. The natural cedar beams and native stone-stacked walls slightly disguised the humble chapel as it blended into the background of the shear side of the mountain. Florence was touched by the peace and natural beauty of the pristine area. She thought how delighted her friend Sister Gratia would be upon seeing it.

Entering the chapel, she appreciated its coolness and soft sand floor. She sat comfortably on a bench and let her mind quieten and open. She felt gratitude for an awareness of the *current of Life* flowing through everything around her. It was like the breeze swaying the leaves of the trees and flowers in the fields. She focused her attention to follow her breaths as they rhythmically slipped through her body, like the underlying heaving of the ocean. Life, living itself, flowing its existence, expressing here and there, upwelling, withdrawing, breathing in and out.

> *Have me flow in Your Divine Flow.*
>
> *Hollow me, a clear reed,*
>
> *Participating in the stream of your force and direction.*
>
> *You, me, us, all, we are You. You are us.*
>
> *The joy of You, the peace of You, gratitude for You.*
>
> *How lucky I am. We are. Thank you.*

Sister Florence sat in happy silence listening to nature's sounds and feeling the late afternoon settle into the shadowing of evening's sunsetting light. Smelling whiffs of the campfire's sweet mesquite smoke, she felt beckoned to her to join her fellow pilgrims.

Juan had hunted a rabbit, as before, and the stew was bubbling. Father Benito restlessly paced back and forth between the campsite and the edge of the canyon, pausing to stare at the plateau on the other side. He could plainly see the cloud of haze now. Its colors were darkening in the dimming rays of the sunset. *He was fighting to distract himself from feeling fearful about the possibilities of what was "over there," waiting for him.*

As the sun finally set behind the tall mountains, they heard the approaching motor of Hans' hummer. Its headlights bobbed in the distance as the car navigated the bumpy desert surface. Coming closer, it pulled up and stopped at the campsite. A sense of comradery diffused through each person as they all bedded down. The slow-moving thicket of stars above, and Hans with one ear open, kept watch over them as they surrendered to the flow of night's time.

Dawn, and Hans, found Father Benito pacing the edge of the canyon searching for the best route to descend and then re-ascend the adjacent plateau. Hans joined Benito. Occasionally, one would point to a low dip on the edge with the other kneeling down to inspect its walkability. Both would eventually shake their heads, no, and move on to other areas. No luck anywhere. When Juan called to them to come to breakfast, remaining puzzled, they momentarily gave up their search.

The Sisters explored the area, delighting in the clear pool, the curved grotto-like rockface of the mountain back-drop, and the little chapel with each rock and cedar log having been lodged in its place with loving care. They were pleasantly surprised by the wild roses blooming profusely in the protected enclosure. Sister Gratia, smiling widely, surveyed it all. Looking up to the sky she said, "And, now, where are You, our dear Lady of Guadalupe?" A flying white turtle dove streaked through the clearing, just missing Gratia's head. Gratia and Florence laughed, calling after it, "Thank you! We know that You are here with us!"

Following breakfast, the men gathered at the edge of the deep arroyo. They were now fully aware of its treacherous quicksand of gravel sides slanting down into the deep bottom of the crevasse. All but Hans indicated that he was feeling drawn to try to cross over to the plateau. The boys periodically dipped a foot down into the loose gravel. *Benito reflected that "Earlier, I thought I would have no interest in the idea of trying to hike over there but, increasingly, I am feeling that I want to go."*

Overhearing this remark, Josie motioned for the Sisters to join the men. Josie addressed them all, saying, "I must remind everyone what my grandmother and mother told me about the plateau. Our Lady told us that only those who had sinned were able to clearly see the plateau. And only they experienced feelings of attraction to try to go there. Those sinners, unfortunately, died during the journey over there like a moth drawn into a flame. Those are the souls who remain trapped in their sins on the plateau. So, be careful. Also, Our Lady invited us to *help her* free the souls. This suggested to me that she already has a plan. But I don't know what it might be."

Father Benito and Hans had been distracted by Josie's talking. Impatiently, after her interruption of their focus on solving the problem of crossing the divide, they resumed their brainstorming. Hans said, "Now here is another idea to try out: Let's use the raft to float on top of the gravel, as on water." He hurried to his hummer shifted his gear and retrieved it. Bringing it to the edge of the ravine, he flipped on its inflator button. Immediately, the raft inflated buoyantly. He fastened a rope into a front top loop and launched the ribbed rubber. It skimmed the gravel surface, sliding down the slope about ten feet, stopping when it reached the end of the rope's length.

"Get on." he said, looking eagerly around at Father and the boys. Everyone hesitated. Sister Florence, looking skeptical quietly offered, "Perhaps a trial run? With a log on top of it?"

Having backed away from the contraption, Benito and the boys quickly agreed and scattered to find a heavy log for the experiment.

Hans selected an appropriate log from those gathered by the boys. Quickly lashing it securely to the raft he again launched the boat now bearing the weight of its log passenger. Excitedly, the boys watched it, silently predicting to themselves if it would, or would not, stay afloat on the deep gravel ocean.

Launched backwards, it slowly slipped downward over the gravel surface. They watched it. It gradually sunk out of sight until it disappeared.

Disappointed and giving up hope for its floatability, Hans watched his rope being pulled downward as if Moby Dick the whale were setting off on it on its own course, trying to tug Hans after it. Hand-over-hand, Hans hauled in the rope. With its attached log cargo, the raft remained submerged, swimming towards them like a submarine, until its nose popped up, scraping the near edge of the crevasse. The boys crowded over the edge lifting the raft up and out of the quicksand of gravel, resting the failed vessel safely on the shore.

The men sat on the bank looking at the unconquerable battlefield. No one offered any additional ideas. But to a man, none was yet willing to give up trying. Perhaps, another day…

The women observing the men looked at each other and shook their heads. They turned towards the pleasant grotto discussing how they could cool off by wading in the pool as they lightly stepped away.

The women decided that they would go swimming in the lovely clear water. They sent Josie to ask the men to stay out of the area for several hours for privacy. Josie did so. The men absent-mindedly agreed as they continued to be deeply engaged in proposing options of how to defeat the gravel graveyard.

Enjoying the peace and quiet of their idyllic setting, the women lost track of time until the sun began to set. They prepared sandwiches for themselves and built a small campfire. They boiled a kettle of hot water and steeped hot tea. Relaxed and contented they watched the stars gradually become visible overhead. Deciding that they wanted to sleep outside of their tent to enjoy the night sky, they tussled their blankets and pillows into pallets on the ground.

They noticed that the eastern horizon began to brighten. Sister Florence remarked, "Is that the sun coming up?" Considering her question for several minutes, Sister Gratia giggled as they watched the full moon rise. They all laughed. Tossing humorous one-liners back and forth, they continued giggling, feeling unrestrained in the privacy of the night. After several lulls between loud giggling episodes, they began to dose.

Until the opening and banging shut of Hans' car doors roused them awake again. The Sisters listened quietly. They heard Hans yell loudly, "More what?" In a slurred voice Benito yelled loudly back, "More wine! White wine! From the sun-ny sho-res of Sic-i-ly. Or, do you have any fi-ne wi-ne from the renown-ed vats of the Benedictine monks on the top of Monte Casino in beautiful I-ta-li- a? T'ador-e, I-ta-li-a!"

There was a long pause while Hans could be heard throwing gear around inside his car. He yelled, "How about some beer?" No answer. Hans, stumbling and kicking rocks, bumped his way back to the dangerous edge of the ravine where the guys had settled down to spend the night. Benito and Hans mumbled to each other as the beer cans' tops popped open.

It grew quiet. The Sisters could hear the crickets resume their night chorusing.

The sound of smacking and crashing broke the silence. Benito, yelled, "What za hell?" Juan, slurring, said, "Gregorio, how big was that one?" Gregorio yelled back, "Ten or fifteen pounds. It didn't sink very fast though." Juan, said, "Try a heavier one!"

The Sisters could hear Benito staggering around stumbling on rocks. Gregorio found a bigger rock and threw it down the ravine. In the moonlight the guys watched it sink into the gravel. Hans slurred, "About twenty-five pounds, for sure! Sank faster than the other one."

Benito commented in a scholarly fashion, "Scientifically, we could accurately calculate both the diameter and weight of a rock by the rate of the speed it sinks. Throw another one, bigger, Gregorio." The women heard a louder crash and splattering gravel. The guys yelled cheers of admiration. Hans challenged them, "Two of you guys, together, what's the biggest rock you can throw in?"

Listening to the guys messing around pushing rocks, grunting, telling one another to "Lift that end, Heave!" the women began to giggle again. Josie began whispering in a heavy Mexican accent and deep voice mocking the boys, repeating their words and grunts. The Sisters uncontrollably laughed loudly, quickly burying their mouths into their pillows trying to muffle their irreverence.

It grew quiet again. The crickets resumed their singing.
Ripping the silence, Benito slurred a scream, "Where's Diego? I counted everyone. He's missing. Oh my God! He's fallen into the arroyo. He's sunk under the gravel! Diego, Diego, where the hell are you, you little ass?"

Juan yelled back at Father Benito, "Here he is, Father. He's asleep on his blanket." Five minutes passed in silence. Benito slurred, "Juan, tell Diego he isn't an ass. Tell him I'm sorry that I called him an ass." Five minutes passed. Benito again yelled, "Juan, did you tell him that? Juan?"

Juan shook Diego, trying to awaken him. Diego yelled, "*Que pasa?*" They argued together. Benito yelled, "Juan did you tell him? What did he say?" Juan yelled back, "He said Is there any more beer?" Hans yelled, "What kind?" Juan yelled, "Cervassa. No gringo beer! Gringo beer makes us throw up. Right Diego? Diego? Diego?"

Benito yelled "Juan, did you tell him that he's not an ass? Tell him I'm sorry that I called him an ass. Diego, you're not a little ass!" Juan in a quieter voice said, "Father, he's asleep."
Finally, the soft sounds of the night breezes in the pines lulled the ghost mountain campers to sleep.

119

CHAPTER EIGHTEEN-THE VIGIL

July

The soft morning light squirmed down through the cottonwood's blowing leaves shifting shadow-patches of shade among the campers. Hans was slowly cooking an aromatic breakfast. Sleepy silence was the only communication among the disheveled loungers as they finished eating their *huevos* and bacon.

Dew on the grasses, roses, and pines in the chapel-grotto area, spurted flashes of jewelry-shine, grabbing the attention of the women who were serenely drinking steaming tea. Inspired, the Sisters began to quietly hum the hymn, Shubert's Ave Maria. Josie joined in harmonizing. Adapting to each other's pitch and key, their voices swelled and flowed into the mesmerizing rhythm of the Latin song, Ave Maria:

Hail Mary, full of grace,
The Lord is with thee,
Blessed art thou among women,
Blessed is the fruit of thy womb, Jesus.
Holy Mary, Mother of God,
Pray for us sinners, now, and,
At the hour of our death. Amen.

The heavenly singing drifted through the men's camp site, over the arroyo, and up the plateau into its mist. It seemed that everything touched by the hymn's hypnotic melody paused and blinked several times. All began waking up, listening, lifting heads, and looking upwards, expectantly.

Father Benito, Hans, and the boys stood up, brushed leaves from their hair, and noticed the stale, after-smell of beer and wine. They scattered to wash-up and refresh themselves back to sober dignity and acceptableness to feminine company.

Abandoning the planning of a frontal attack on the Battlefield of the Sinking Gravel, and attracted by the inspiring

120

singing, they gathered at the chapel. Father Benito asked Josie to again relate the information given by her women relatives. And just what it was that Our Lady was wanting of them?

Josie recounted the main parts of the story. Benito had been listening carefully. "Josie, what was it that you said yesterday? *The part about Our Lady wanting us to help her with a plan that she already has?"* Josie shook her head, "I don't really know what it is. She led me to understand only that she very much wanted to free the trapped souls and wanted us to help her." In silence, Benito and the others considered Josie's information.

The thought came to him to ask Sister Gratia. She had been silently praying for guidance. She quietly responded, "I belong to the nuns' Order of Divine Mother, devoted to honoring the Blessed Mother Mary. Through experience, we have found that She indeed is active in bringing salvation to souls.

"In the realm of the Communion of the Saints, she has a tradition of communicating her plans and wishes to those who listen to her and who have a desire to join her in the work of bringing salvation to souls. She makes appearances in visions, inspires music, dances, art and architecture, dictates writings, conveys thoughts of guidance, feelings of comfort and hope, and when requested, *'Prays for us, now, and at the hour of our death. Amen.'*

"To your inquiry of 'what does she want from us,' Father Benito, perhaps, what we can do is to *ask to have a listening receptive willingness* to be guided by her. A word of warning though. Through the experience of those of us within the nuns' Order of The Divine Mother, 'Be careful of what you ask for.'

"You see, the spiritual way things work is holistically. That is, when one asks to help another, Our Lady's plan includes, not only helping the other, but during the process, also, helping the Asker, who is You. The Asker is thrown into the adventure of being helped, too. And that frequently means experiencing deep changes of spiritual growth within yourself. These changes can be very humbling, disturbing, frightening, threatening, as well as, joyfully ecstatic.

'Often, there is this tumultuous nature of being guided by Our Lady. That is why certain called seekers come together. We need the mutual understanding and support, personally, as well as in our TDY (temporary duty) service missions. We receive this help from Grace within the Community dynamics of our religious order of Divine Mother. Community is essential. Grace is essential." Finished, Sister Gratia excused herself and entered the chapel to pray.

In silence, again considering their situation in the light of what Sister Gratia shared, Benito realized that to work with Our Lady required a new approach. He could now see that to traverse the ravine of the dead was not a material challenge but one in the spiritual realm. The image came to him of the ancient legend of Charon poling his boat crossing the River Styx transporting the souls of the deceased over into the land of the dead, Hades.

It occurred to him that he had additional problems with this situation. He needed to think through all this stuff. Turing to Sister Florence, he asked her to take a walk with him "to figure things out." She nodded. As they left the group, the boys decided to take a swim and splashed into the cool clean water.

Benito and Florence walked pensively among the pine trees along the base of the mountains. Stopping to rest, they sat on the soft fallen pine needles. Benito said in a quiet honest tone, "I don't really believe that there is a spiritual realm. It's not scientific at all. It's just superstition, invented by scared people who find themselves in desperate circumstances." After a long pause, he continued, "Up until now I've gotten by fine not having to openly 'believe' in a spiritual realm of existence. I did my jobs well. No one confronted me about 'believing'.

"Two things: One, I instinctively have concentrated on allowing parishioners to have their socializing or community as Sister Gratia called it. I understood the importance of that from growing up in my Italian Family. Two, I had a dream the other night about feeling very happy and satisfied about pleasing my Italian Family by achieving the building of a church and orphanage and becoming a bishop. They expect that of me to be

122

a success like that. That type of success reflects upon their success as a mob Family. I think that I can probably achieve those things, too. After deciding to take that route, talking to the archbishop's assistant, I felt a let-down. No interest in it. No motivation. That surprised me. *But, now, in what direction do I go?* "Sister Florence was quietly listening to him. She could hear his creeping pessimism.

"I guess the thing for me to do is to pack up, end this camping trip, give my fancy expensive black car a good wash, wax, and polish, and return to my job in D.C. Even though it is just an eight to five job, it pays pretty well. And my Family will just have to be disappointed in me, eh?"

Benito picked up a pine cone and threw it as far as he could from his sitting-down position. He remained sitting, dejectedly looking into the distance across the wide expanse of desert shrub and sand stretching as far as the eye could see.

Finally, Sister Florence stood up, turned to look at him sitting, slumping, on the ground and said, "Chicken! I can smell your fear. I would like to see you 'Man Up!' *Take a risk and* see what Our Lady (if she exists for you) has in store for you. Why she drew you here."

Walking away, she called back to him Shakespeare's quote from Hamlet, "There are more things in heaven and earth, Horatio, than are dreamt of in your philosophy". Benito felt his fear punch him in his stomach. The Jericho walls of his safe world were tumbling down.

Returning to the campsite, Benito wandered to the edge of the ravine surveying the plateau. He thought, "I know that it is just a very high pile of rocks with a cloud of semi-condensed water vapor on the top of it. A crowd of ghosts trapped up there! Sure!" He chuckled sarcastically. He sat down, picked up small pebbles within reach and absentmindedly tossed them over the edge down into the graveled abyss.

Florence had re-joined Josie who was hand-flattening flour and corn masa into tortillas. Josie motioned to Diego. He maneuvered two stout sticks and pulled a heated stone with a wide flat surface out of the fire and into her kitchen area. She slapped the rounded dough pieces onto the hot surface, smiling as they baked golden brown.

Gregorio had hunted out a three-foot-long log of soft white pine. He was artistically carving it into the likeness of Our Lady of Guadalupe. Juan was inspecting, repairing, and improving the stone and cedar log chapel. Gratia and Hans were rearranging the gear in the hummer, chatting pleasantly.

Florence noticed Benito contemplating the abyss and walked his way. Seeing her slowly approaching, he squirmed uncomfortably. He recognized how dissatisfied with himself he felt. As she sat down beside him, he spilled out, "Okay, okay. I get it!"

Looking up at the sky, addressing Our Lady, he talked to her saying, "I want to help you with your plan to free the trapped souls! *I am willing!*"

Re-considering he murmured, "If there are any such things as trapped souls on top of a mountain." He finally added, "Our Lady, I need your help in this. Please."

Holding still, they listened. They could hear only the wind occasionally brush through the tops of the pine trees. Sister Florence reached over and patted his hand, smiling. She told him sincerely, "And remember Benito, no matter what happens, Sister Gratia and I will be holding on to you in our prayers and with our love. We will not let you fall away. Be brave and grow spiritually as much as you can." Pausing and looking at him with respect and compassion, she said softly, "Good luck."

CHAPTER NINETEEN-AWAKENING

July

Josie sent Diego to invite them all to a home-cooked meal with fresh-baked tortillas. Following lunch, it was siesta time. Relaxing around the pool in the shade, the women began again to gently sing the Ave Maria as a meditative prayer to Our Lady of Guadalupe.

Hearing the women sweetly singing the song-phrase pleading to Our Lady, "Pray for us, now, and at the hour of our death.", Father Benito was touched in his heart by the memory of the disappointed face of *Abuela*. Her tragic expression, "The hour of *her* death", the *dying of her hope* of receiving Her Lord, Her Life. A murder caused by his refusal to administer communion which led to the death of her human life soon thereafter.

Overcome with compassion and grief he began to cry. Slumping to his knees, he raised his head to the misted plateau. In the haze of his suffering, he began to walk on his knees towards the arroyo speaking sadly, "I, too, am a sinner. I belong over there to suffer with the others who have sinned like me. Here I am, here I am, here I am…." Repeating the words of his condemnation of himself to the hell of entrapment in suffering, he approached the edge of the gravel slope.

Alarmed, the men rushed towards him, tackling him from behind and dragged him away from that crevasse that sinks all things. Sitting slumped forward where they dropped him, he continued to whimper. Remaining in a daze, he slowly rose to his knees and repeated his attempt to journey to the edge. Again, the men dragged him back. This time, Hans used his long rope to tie Benito's foot to the cottonwood tree. Benito continued whimpering, enclosed in his world of suffering. He methodically tugged on the rope, wanting to cross the abyss to join the trapped souls on the top of La Place de las Animas.

Seeing Father Benito acting like he was out of his mind, caused the boys to feel disturbed. They withdrew a distance from him. Hans took it in stride having seen men shocked from combat act quite strangely. He worked nearby restoring his raft's inflating mechanism. The women came near to Benito and sat in vigil, singing and praying together for him and his mission of freeing the trapped souls.

Lulled by their own chanting, the Sisters began to doze. Hans absorbed himself in his preoccupation with the raft. The boys deliberately were elsewhere. Benito remained in his dazed state of mind, suffering and continually tugging at the rope tied to the tree. The rope eventually loosened its knot, slipping away from the tree trunk.

Free, Benito dragged the long rope tied to his ankle behind him along the ground and walked himself on his knees towards the steep edge. He was lost in the mumbling of his confession of guilt and crying. Reaching the sharp drop-off, he step-kneeled himself over. Slowly sinking down into the loose gravel as in quicksand. He thrashed his hands and arms trying to stay afloat, crashing and scattering pebbles.

Startled by the commotion, Hans leaped forward barely able to grab the end of the rope before it snaked down under the gravel following Benito's sinking body. Looking over the edge, Hans saw Benito's curly black head submerge. He had slid about ten feet down the slope. Crawling into a sitting position, Hans braced his outstretched legs and feet against a boulder. He began pulling the rope in hand over hand. Benito remained submerged. Desperately, Hans pulled faster until the rope snagged, coming to an abrupt halt.

Hans yelled out in frustration, flapping the rope up and down, attempting to unsnag it. The boys came running. Seeing the situation, they yelled encouragement, "Pull harder! Don't give up, Father! Damn, damn, damn! Let me try to pull it!" The women prayed harder, squinting their eyes shut and begging for help to save Father Benito.

All their efforts could not retrieve Father Benito. Hans possessively held on to the rope. He was mentally back in combat on the battlefield holding onto his wounded Buddy, determined to use his entire self, willing to give up his own life to save his fellow soldier. Hans tied the end of the rope around his wrist. He continued to flap it up and down, in this and that direction, sideways, vertically. Tears trickled down his cheeks. In a low voice, he chanted, "Come on, unsnag! Come on, unsnag! ...."

Minutes passed. Juan swore that he saw the gravel move and Father's nose poke up to take a breath. More minutes passed. Juan swore that he saw the same thing happen again. Then later, again. More minutes passed. They began to wonder, "How long can this go on?" No one was willing to think beyond the present or to even consider stopping the vigil for Father Benito's life.

The women began to sing again, Ave Maria. Their song was infused with their desperate praying and mentally and spiritually holding onto Father Benito's life. Sister Florence sent him mental messages, "We're here, Benito. We're holding on to you. We won't let go of you. Come back to us when you are ready. Our love is holding on to you. Hold on to us. Be brave. Finish your mission. Follow the guidance of Our Lady. We're here. We're here ...."

Meanwhile, Father Benito began to realize that he was in a daze of his self-imposed suffering of guilt and self-condemnation. He paused and observed his dazed state of mind, trying to figure out where he was and what was happening to him. Everything was dark. The thought came to him that he had agreed to help Our Lady of Guadalupe to free the trapped souls. Perhaps, his situation, now, had to do with that? As he had the thought of wanting to ask her, she mentally spoke to him.

"Benito? Yes, this me. My identity is *The Divine Mother.* I am the aspect of God that is the feminine. I am the divine force of life that is born, or manifests, in all created things. Throughout history I have revealed myself to people in many different manifestations. I am called the Fertility Goddess, the multiple Hindu female goddesses, the Blessed Virgin Mary, and many other names in many other cultures. I am the force that is Wisdom, Spirit, nurturing and caring, growth, kindness, acceptance, compassion, and unconditional love.

I am Our Lady of Carmel that your Italian people in Chicago received encouragement, guidance, and strength from in their early years of their struggles when settling there. I want you to know, my beloved child, that just as I loved them dearly, now, with your foot snagged in a rock crevice like a snagged fish on a line, *you are dearly loved by me!*" Like nothing he had ever experienced before, Benito felt an ecstasy of Our Lady's love engulf him. Within the gushing of his tears, a love awakened in his heart. A surge of gratitude welled up within him. *His world changed,* in a twinkling of an eye.

She continued, "Yes, you are submerged under the sea of gravel and barely able to breathe. You are not dead. You are having a near-death experience. It is not your time to die. Your work over there is not yet finished. Although, whether you remain trapped with the other souls here, or return, depends on your own efforts. I am allowing you this opportunity to help me free the trapped souls here as you told me that you so desire. One's free will and desires must always be permitted to happen. Dealing with the consequences of one's choices takes up most of one's time while on earth.

"I am allowing Sister Gratia to listen in and observe what is happening to you. I want her to record all of it plus I am revealing much more to her to share with my beloved seekers. It will be one of my gifts to them, my response to their requests for further guidance in their spiritual growth.

"However, you will have little memory of these details. But this event will remain with you, incorporated as an experience of spiritual growth. It will be a deep well of living water for you to draw upon to help others. Do you understand?" Benito indicated that he did.

Benito asked, "What is your plan to free the trapped souls? Why are they even here, trapped?"

Our Lady replied, "These souls have sinned. That's why they are here, trapped. They must experience several steps in spiritual growth in order to choose to free themselves. That is where you come in. Along with those others who are in vigil praying for you and sending you love and caring about the progress of your soul's growth."

Benito replied, "Let's do it. How do we start?"

Our Lady said, "You have already taken some of the steps: You have let yourself acknowledge and realize your sin of destroying *Abuela's* hope of being loved unconditionally by her beloved Lord through receiving him in communion. You admit that you did this when you let yourself be intimidated by the white parishioners with their racism. And you just didn't *care* about *Abuela* or about anyone else in your parish. Next, you have now embraced the virtues of compassion and caring and let yourself feel and share *Abuela's* grief and loss.

The next required step is for you is to make amends, and, in the future, to act with sensitivity and respect for others' hopes and to show them empathy as they struggle.

"How do you think that you can do that?"

Father Benito became tearful. He confessed that it was now impossible to make amends to *Abuela* since she was dead.

Our Lady responded, "Oh, is she? Look over there." The ghostly form of *Abuela* appeared, smiling and glowing with a happy warmth of love.

Mentally, Benito fell on his knees, kneel-walking towards her. Reaching down he barely lifted the hem of her skirt made of golden light and kissed it. Crying, he apologized to her and begged for her forgiveness. Surprised, he felt that she was feeling only love for him.

Our Lady said "It was *Abuela's* wish that you be brought here for the gift of this experience. She wanted to act so that others like herself when she was on earth would be spared such suffering and despair as she endured at your hands. She has prayed constantly for your spiritual growth in this area. She hopes that you take advantage of this opportunity." Smiling at him, the form of *Abuela* faded away.

Deeply touched by the love Abuela was carrying for him, even after he had hurt her, Benito was filled with gratitude.

Benito felt that he was a changed and better man. He was eager to perform acts of love to others such as he had just experienced.

Our Lady told him, "You will be allowed to have that chance since you are desiring it.

"My plan is that you cross over to the plateau and minister to the trapped souls by passing on to them what you just experienced. Draw upon the prayers and support of those keeping vigil for your success. We are all connected. When one of us is loved, we are all loved. When one of us is unloved, all of us are unloved.

"Benito, at your stage of spiritual growth, what is needed is for you to apply through actions with zeal your empathy and compassion for *others' hope of being loved unconditionally.* How you do this is your particular challenge during this lifetime. You are to expect, notice, and accept the tools of Grace and Community. These are the gifts of Heaven on Earth."

Mentally, Benito was whisked across the abyss into the mist of the plateau and found himself being stared at by a multitude of ghostly eyes. Welling up within his soul, he experienced feelings of kinship with each set of suffering eyes.

He felt strength from the upwelling of support and prayer from his friends below keeping vigil for him and his mission to free these trapped souls. He felt *Abuela's* love and encouragement.

Then he felt a powerful surge of loving golden light shining through him as if he were a flashlight. It was the overwhelming presence of Our Lady of Guadalupe's unconditional love for these struggling souls. She had never given up on even one of them.

He floated through the throng, reaching out and holding each one's precious cheeks between his palms, gazing at them, letting Our Lady beam her unconditional love through him into their tortured tired hearts. One by one, they transfigured into golden columns of light. They streaked like meteorites across a dark sky in ecstasy, experiencing *the freedom of being dearly loved,* on their ways to pass on to others the Love that they had just received.

Suddenly the rope jerked Benito's foot free from the rock cleft. Hans reeled in his big fish. The boys whooped with joy. They reached down and pulled out Father's body, bobbing like a slippery fish. "Is he breathing? Is anything broken? Is he still in a daze? Is he awake? Father Benito? BENITO! Are you alright?"

Sitting up and looking around at each one of his friends, Benito smiled with joy and said, "I love you, and you, and you … Thank you, thank you.

"Let's go. I've got work to do."

WHERE
Standing on bare rock,
High swirling wind,
Whipping her long hair,
Searching among far away peaks,
Smeared in her tears.

Her crying sprayed outward her wet demand,
For an answer:
Is there anyone,
Who loves me,
For who I am?

CHAPTER TWENTY-HOMES

August

Many miles and hours later, the small caravan pulled into Elena's yard long after dark. Sister Florence and Father Benito dreaded what would happen when the boys met Diego's "mother." Letting the boys enter the house first, like cowards, the priest and nun remained in the car. The initial disappointment, disillusionment, and anger that Diego felt was brief.

Elena smoothed over the situation by explaining that what had happened were choices of "practical solutions" to their life-threatening circumstances. She reframed their present relationships as being "lucky" that they, at least, had each other, especially, now that little Mari was here with them.

She stated that each person was to adjust to "make the best of things." She said there were going to be many problems that lay ahead for each of them but together they were to protect and accept each other as family as they worked hard to "help out" each other in every way that they could. They were to find work and bring in money for their "family." They were to help out with the household chores and, of course, take care of Mari, helping her to feel safe. Elena then took a deep breath and said, "Welcome home!" passing around a huge platter of steaming hot tamales.

Inside the small two-bedroom house, the boys bedded down wherever they could. Sleeping soundly, they were glad to be "home." Benito and Hans drove the rest of their group to the local motel for the night, rejoining civilization once more.

The next day was Sunday. From the motel the group walked to the café at the gas station. They found seating at their previous booth. Their fragrant orders of fresh cooked pancakes and omelets were served with glasses of red tomato and yellow orange juices. Setting on the shiny white table top, the juice colors sparkled in the morning sunlight streaming through the plate glass window.

Father Benito contemplated their setting. Silently a prayer of gratitude swelled up from his heart. Smiling at his friends sharing this breakfast with him, he was happy. He felt loved and cared about. Following breakfast, glancing around the café, he again noticed the elderly woman sitting alone. Woodrow's wife, Irene. He observed that the bitter, racist, intimidating spokesperson for the white parish was now revealed to be fragile and withdrawn, eating by herself on a Sunday morning.

Taking his coffee mug, he excused himself and made his way over to her booth. "Excuse me. Mrs. Smith? I am Father Benito, the pastor of the former Catholic parish. Do you remember me? May I join you?" Initially puzzled, she slowly smiled and then motioned for him to sit down. His caring interaction with her seemed to energize her and she became more talkative and animated. She took hold of his hand, pumping it up and down on the table, in rhythm with their conversation. Looking at each other, they mutually understood that she did not want to let go of him.

In silence, she began tearing up. Empathizing with her feelings, he remained with her, supportively returning her grasp on his hand. Recovering with a weak smile, she said in a tentative tone, "I don't suppose that you would come to my house for an afternoon tea today?" Looking at his group of friends making their way out to the cars in the parking lot, he quickly considered and replied, "Yes, let's have tea together this afternoon. Thank you. May I bring someone with me?" Giving him a grateful and happy face, she shook her head with a big Yes!

The boys had cleaned and polished his handsome black Cadillac to a high shine. Grinning, they escorted him with Rosa and Mari at his side into his chariot for his afternoon tea date. Rosa had taken some convincing to agree to go. She assumed her suspicious hyper-vigilant attitude towards her surroundings as they drove through town, arriving at the big house. It was situated in the middle of a homestead within a five-acre landscaped lawn. The curving driveway led them to the rear of the grand house to the garden cottage. This was now the efficiency residence of the grand lady of the house. She was waiting for them as she stood waving behind the wooden screen of the front door.

Watching them get out of the car and seeing little Mari, whatever remnants of former unkindness Irene may have been holding in her heart, melted like ice cubes in the warmth of sunshine. Irene couldn't stop smiling and cooing, "Ohhhh, ohhh, what a little darling. Ohhh."

Father helped Irene into her wheelchair. He pushed while she gave them a tour of her farmstead: the yard, shaded with large sycamores, pecans, elms, persimmons, and cottonwood trees, the old barn and chicken house, and, finally the inside of the big house. Mari was energetically playing and exclaiming, "Mama, look at this!" as she explored everything they came upon. She also kept her Mommy within sight at all times. Fully furnished, Irene's home had ten bedrooms and five bathrooms, a large kitchen, dining room, two living rooms, front and back porches, and several smaller multi-use rooms downstairs and up. Irene reminisced about the happier times and events that had occurred in the various rooms.

They returned to her cottage and settled her into her rocking chair. Rosa served her some refreshments. As Benito prepared to soon leave, Irene concluded, "Thank you for letting me share the commentary of my life with you, Father. I have outlived everyone in my family and most of my friends. No one from my former life is left."

After holding his hand for a long time, she squeezed it good-bye. Rosa helped Mari give her a hug to Irene's delight. They waved each other good bye as Benito slowly drove out of the winding driveway.

Irene had a peaceful night's rest, the first in a long time. She felt a sense of wellbeing, grateful to have had the opportunity to be around people who cared about her. She wanted to do it again, soon.

The next morning, she sent her gardener with a message to

Father Benito. After lunch he arrived in his fine car. Inviting him into her living area, she became serious. "Father, something has been bothering me for a long time. May I talk to you about it?" Gently he agreed. They sat at her round kitchen table. She began, "Do you remember that Sunday a long time ago during Mass when that old *Mesican* woman came kneel-walking down the aisle?" Irene looked at him nervously. Benito silently nodded his head, yes.

Irene continued, "Well, this a hard subject for me to talk about. I'm not sure how to feel about it. Can you tell me, was it a sin for me to have insisted that you turn her away from receiving communion?" Making no sounds, Irene was unaware that she was working her mouth anxiously, quickly glancing at him, turning away from him, then glancing at him again. She was obviously upset at the memory which she had probably re-churned in her mind many times over. Benito realized that she was suffering from her guilty conscience. He could relate to her pain as he himself had felt the same.

Closing his eyes, he silently asked Our Lady to put this suffering soul into her hands and to use him as she would to help Irene grow spiritually. Softly, Benito shared with Irene, "Yes, it was a sin. What you did, and what I did, deeply hurt that *Abuela*. She later died from it. She interpreted my refusal to administer communion to her as her Lord rejecting her. She suffered a broken heart."

Together they were quiet. Irene then asked, "Father will you hear my confession? Now? Here?" Benito reached into his cassock pocket, pulled out his purple stole, unrolled it and placed it around his neck. They bowed their heads. Irene said, "Bless me Father, for I have sinned. My last confession was a long time ago. I have sinned by hating that *Mesican* old woman and causing her to die of a broken heart. I am sorry." At that she broke into tears as the tragedy of what she had done overwhelmed her.

Father sat compassionately with her through her grieving. After she had somewhat collected herself, he reached across the

135

table and held her hand. They both soaked up the human comfort of needing to have shared with each other. He proceeded to complete administering to her the Sacrament of Reconciliation, absolving her from her sins and blessing her with the sign of the cross.

Father stood up, asking Irene if he might brew a cup of tea for them and serve a snack. She gratefully pointed to the kitchen cabinets and tea kettle. Placing the refreshments on a tray, they moved into the living room area and sat in comfortable chairs to enjoy a peaceful break.

Irene said matter-of-factly to Benito, "Father, you did not give me a penance. What should I do?" Benito smiled, considering her question. "We know *Abuela* has passed. But she has an *adopted granddaughter* who might benefit from some act of inclusion and kindness from you." With her interest piqued, Irene asked, "Who in the world is it and where in the world would I find her?" In a matter-of-fact tone he replied, "You met her yesterday. Her name is Mariposa, a beautiful little butterfly who lives on the Mexican side of town.'"

Surprised, Irene's face brightened. "This reminds me of the old days when our church women's Sunday School group were given the name of a needy family. We did a good job of gathering groceries and delivering a basket onto their doorstep." Her voice had taken on the sound of dedication and competency. She looked blankly at Benito, waiting for his go-ahead.

Thoughtfully Benito gently suggested, "Let's try something a little different this time, Irene. Something that is more closely an action to make amends for your sin, our sin. Perhaps, an act of kindness that conveys to little Mari that you want to include, not exclude, or hate, her. Something just between the two of you. Something to let her know that she is personally loved, accepted, and wanted. Something that is the opposite of what *Abuela* felt." Benito paused.

Irene was at a loss. "Why, I have no idea what would make those people feel that way." She shook her head, puzzled, and looked out the window. Father smiled kindly at her. "Let's think about it. And let's ask Our Lady of Guadalupe for ideas. Okay?" He stirred. preparing to leave. Frustrated, Irene shifted in her chair with a frown on her face. She did not like leaving problems unsolved.

Pulling forward in her chair, she indicated that she wasn't finished talking to him. Irene changed the subject asking him to please stay a little while longer. Hesitating, he agreed and sat back in his chair waiting for her to continue. Lifting her cell phone from the end table, she clumsily punched in a phone number. Holding the phone to her ear briefly, she spoke, "Yes, George, it's me. I'm ready now, come on in. Yes, the front door is open. Yes, now. Bring the paperwork. Yes, we're ready."

Gathering her thoughts, she was quiet. Momentarily, George tapped on the front door and let himself in. An elderly fellow, he still dressed professionally in a business suit. He formerly greeted Mrs. Smith and introduced himself to Benito who stood to shake hands with him. Sitting at the nearby kitchen table, George set his briefcase down and opened its lid. He removed papers and stacked them in orderly piles. Papers prepared, he deferred to Irene to explain the proceedings.

Watching George, Irene was deep in serious thought. She intentionally turned to Benito, cleared her throat, and slowly explained to him, "Father Benito, I want George my longtime family attorney to witness the agreements and terms that we are now discussing. I am requesting that you agree to serve as the beneficiary of my estate. I am conveying my entire estate to you of my free will with no coercion and am of sound mind. I have no living heirs, so I am free of any family obligations and customary inheritance practices.

"My final wishes are that the estate be conveyed to you alone in your name with no claims to it by the Catholic Church or any other organization. There are to be no restrictions or limitations on your use of any part of the estate. You alone are the sole designated beneficiary. You are free to legally transact any and all parts of the estate for any purpose at any time as you see fit.

"The transfer into your name and control of the entire estate, all the assets of a monetary nature and of a real estate nature, and all other individual items, is to take place today upon your agreement and with the placement of your notarized signature on the appropriate documents.

I do request that I be allowed to remain in this cottage residence and receive a monthly stipend until the day of my death."

Becoming silent she turned to George asking him if she had left out anything. He smiled and shook his head, no. She turned to Benito and asked him if he had any questions.

Benito wondered if he had heard her correctly. He did not know what to say. George arose from his chair, officially addressing the priest, "Father Benito, do you agree to the terms expressed here of your own free will with no coercion and being of sound mind? If so, please step forward and sign these documents so indicating."

Seeing his inaction, Irene pressed him. "Benito! Say the word, Yes!" Benito slowly pronounced the requested word: "Yes." Looking at her, humbly, Benito softly added with deep respect and gratitude, "Thank you, Irene." George motioned him forward as Benito stood. Feeling slightly numb, Benito dutifully signed all the papers.

Their business completed, George shook his hand, wished him good luck, and invited him to call on him for assistance with any legal issues, at any time. He handed over his card and a packet of legal papers containing the details of the estate. Irene thanked George as he made his way out.

Benito and Irene looked at each other feeling a comforting closeness. He did not know what to say. Seeing that Benito was still stunned, she took hold of his hand and squeezed into it a ring of keys. Guiding him to the door and smiling at him, she said, "It's a lot to think about. I recommend that you move into the front, south-facing bedroom. It gets a good breeze and has wonderful light. Feel free to come in and out anytime. Oh! And there are several million dollars in the accounts. It is all yours now."

Closing the door behind him, she leaned against it and let out a big sigh of relief saying, "Now, I don't have to worry about anything! Except what kindness to gift to that little *Mesican* girl to carry out my assigned penance."

CHAPTER TWENTY-ONE-IRENE

August

Asking to speak privately with Sister Florence, Benito invited her to accompany him on a drive through the neighborhoods of the town. He related all the details of becoming Irene's estate beneficiary. She shared his shock and surprise at each part of the story. He drove them past the farmstead pointing out the various structures to her. She was impressed by the size of the house and wondered aloud what he could do with all of it. He related that the monetary assets amounted to several million dollars. The whole thing seemed unreal to both of them. Considering his many possibilities, he stated, "Why I could not only buy my bishopric but a cardinal title too."

He asked Sister Florence what she would like to see him do with the estate. Hesitating, she admitted, "Benito, I have no idea what you should do with it. What an interesting twist this is along your path. This is yet another new beginning for you. I wonder if Our Lady of Guadalupe is behind this and, if so, what are her plans for you? So much is happening to you! What did Gratia say? 'Be careful what you ask for ….,' when dealing with Our Lady. And I've noticed that the hair around your temples turned grey after your ordeal back at the plateau." Seeing his concerned look as he viewed himself in the rearview mirror, she quickly added, "But grey temples look handsome on a man." Catching her humor, he grinned.

Her words reminded Benito that his new path of spiritual growth now required him to frequently turn to Our Lady for guidance. To be able do this he needed to seek out peaceful circumstances and time to listen, meditate, and pray. Otherwise, he was falling back into his old habit of trying to muscle himself forward, close-mindedly seeking to accomplish his own little ideas and goals, and stubbornly insisting on everyone doing everything his way.

Blessed with a new-found insight, he was beginning to recognize the differences between trying to operate in the

140

spiritual realm versus the material realm. He was trying to adjust his desires for accomplishments away from those that were concrete and visible to accomplishments within the realm of peoples' soul-growth.

He preferred to experience those feelings of happiness and joy that came when the people he was interacting with made spiritual breakthroughs. He deeply appreciated and enjoyed the feelings of gratitude to Our Lady that welled-up within him at those times. He wanted to live in that realm of love and joy forever.

He shared with Florence, "The first thing that I want to do is to use the homestead for a retreat refuge, a place of peace to allow me and others to commune with Our Lady. Florence, would you and Sister Gratia, and Hans go with me to the homestead tomorrow and see about setting up that environment? And maybe Elena's family would enjoy a picnic on the place too. And, Irene." Sister Florence consented and observed that nuns' Order of the Divine Mother had set up their own retreat center camp located in the lovely hill country area of Texas. She continued, "It's very helpful and necessary to have a peaceful place of recollection. A very good idea, Benito. Yes, that is an excellent place to start." After a silent pause, she added, "Benito, before you make any decisions about this, perhaps we need to not tell anyone about your estate. Just keep it private." Benito gave a sigh of relief. "The same thought had just occurred to me too. Let's just you and I drive out to the homestead and inspect it. Maybe we could visit with Irene to learn more about what else is there and about the conditions of the structures, for example. Would you help me do that, please?" Smiling, Florence agreed.

The next morning, Irene, standing at the kitchen counter, picked up the handle of her single-cup-coffee-maker pot, ready to pour the freshly brewed steaming, French-vanilla flavored, black gold into her fine china cup. First, she raised the pot and said to the ceiling "How about sharing a cup of this 'good-morning' with me, Father Benito? And bring that sweet baby, too, for some hot chocolate. Yes, tell her it has tiny marshmallows floating in it." Smiling, she continued and poured her own cup almost to the rim, thinking, "Not too full, again, Irene. Your shaky hand will get you another hot splash-bath." Hearing the soft crunch of driveway gravel, she looked out the kitchen window and saw the shiny black Cadillac arriving. Grinning on her way to open the front door, she thought, "How powerful is that! Think of Benito and he appears! You've got some strong voo-doo going, old gal!"

Opening the door, she was greeted by a grinning handsome man with curly black hair now turned grey around his temples. From behind his back, he pulled out a bouquet of red roses and presented them to her with a hand flourish. Pushing open the wooden screen door, she laughed a musical spontaneous light-hearted laugh. Suddenly realizing that she had not laughed in what seemed like years, she teared up with feelings of gratitude for this moment, for *all* of this, for her life, for now.

She was pleased to meet Sister Florence. Irene agreed to accompany them into the big house for another tour. Sitting in her wheelchair, Benito pushed her up the ramp into the living room. She directed him to the master bedroom with its full bath, *en suite*, that she was recommending to him to use for his own quarters. It was furnished with a heavy rich brown walnut bedroom set. The queen-size bed was made up with clean fresh linens. She said, "It's all ready for you to move into. All the bedrooms are ready to use. And the bathrooms. The kitchen is stocked. I keep them that way just in case I would have some company drop in. I employ a yard man and housekeeper full-time. I have always believed in keeping up in good condition everything that I own. Learned that in the depression, when whatever we were lucky enough to have, we took good care of it because it had to last. Benito, I hope that you will do the same. But now that's up to you and I trust you to do what's best from here on out." She took hold of his hand and squeezed it, smiling up at him. He squeezed back and returned her smile with fondness.

Exploring the kitchen, Florence found the twelve-cup glass

pot Mr. Coffee maker and a fresh unopened package of dark roast medium ground coffee. Indicating her find, she asked if anyone would like a cuppa? They nodded their heads eagerly, yes. Further exploring the insides of the cabinets, she discovered a package of waffle style ice-cream cookies with cream fillings of assorted flavors of vanilla, strawberry, and chocolate. In the adjacent dining room, she approached a china cabinet and buffet side-board. Slightly stooping she examined the china cabinet's treasures and drew out a fragile antique plate of a light-green color intricately etched depression glass with fluted edges. Setting it carefully on the kitchen cabinet, she arranged the cookies on it in a star-burst design. She was having fun playing house. Irene caught Sister Florence's eyes. They giggled at each other, sharing, that as two women, they both appreciated Irene's fine china and her well-provisioned home. Florence served them at the small kitchen table. They relaxed into the padded captain chairs on wheels which Irene easily maneuvered.

Feeling the peace and pleasantness of Irene's lovely home they quietly enjoyed it. They couldn't help but smile at each other, at their hot coffee, at…. everything around them. Gazing at Irene, Benito felt deep gratitude for her. He recognized that he was developing an appreciation for her wisdom and foresight. He was feeling a respect for her strength as a woman, managing her extensive estate affairs, all within a man's world of rules made for men's benefits. And she was doing a good job of it.

Putting down his coffee cup and addressing Irene respectfully he politely asked, "Irene, Sister Florence and I are beginning to explore how I might use your gift of your estate. Would you consider joining us in evaluating the possibilities, please? I would appreciate you sharing your wisdom and experiences with me in helping make these decisions." Irene directed her attention to him full-face with a non-comital expression.

Passing through her mind came recollections of her former business dealings with men. She, like all women of her time, and living on the farm, had learned to develop skills and strategies to interact with men. She had learned the early lessons of needing to de-value and hide her true talents and abilities while trying to inflate the values and egos of the men.

This antic had to be combined with sly manipulations of the men into thinking that her best ideas were their own. The next challenge was to ensure that the actions needed to carry out the plans actually happened. This required an array of tasks and strategies including arranging work events with home-made pies; teaching the how-to's; gathering the necessary materials and tools; constantly puffing up the men's egos, sometimes through using out-right lies; implying that motivating rewards lay close ahead, which might include sex. All of this, "dancing backwards, and in high-heels" had to be pulled off with no appearances of nagging, controlling, being more powerful than men, and, definitely not being smarter or more competent than they were. And when all else failed she would need to get up early, at the last minute, and do the tasks all by herself. This last-ditch solution she sometimes discovered later was the men's own strategy all along.

Irene remembered most of all how exhausting was that process of working with men. And how her required deviousness had left such a bad taste in her mouth. She thought, No. No thanks. I am through with having to ever do that again, thank goodness! And thank goodness that I am old and can gracefully get away with saying, No!

Shaking her head, No, she put herself down demurely for the last time by meekly saying, "Reverend Father Benito, you are so smart. You are the best one for making the estate decisions. The outdated opinions of this old lady couldn't possibly be of any value to anyone. But, thank you for asking me." Staring down at the cookie plate she withdrew into her demeaned self. She carefully tried to control her shaky hand by using both hands to grasp the cup while she finished drinking her coffee. She felt that

144

she had paid her last dues of performing her role as a mere woman who was destined to be subservient to men as was required by her time in history. Going forward she felt free to be her real self. Finally!

CHAPTER TWENTY-TWO-BUILDING

August

Father Benito announced to the town, "Mrs. Smith is letting me use and take care of her homestead." He invited them to come over for a picnic and to bring their families and friends. "And bring a covered dish if anyone wants to but there will be plenty of food for everyone." Benito asked Hans and Elena to organize everything. He opened a charge account at the Walmart store and gave them a budgeted amount to "buy whatever they needed." Hans and Elena made out lists, visited the farmhouse facilities, and planned the menu. They visited with the housekeeper, Donna, and the yardman, Franco, coordinating the hiring of extra staff. They made rental arrangements with an entertainment company to provide an inflatable bounce house for the kids and hired a local band which played Mexicana music. They hired a Hispanic food catering company. Elena asked Rosa if Mari had ever had a *piñata?* No. So, they arranged to have several of them made and hung in the trees. Their festive mood was contagious. Soon the boys were asking if there could be a four-wheeler rented for them to ride? And a soccer goal-kicking contest set up? And Juan loudly suggested let's bring in a bull and have a bull fight!

Meanwhile, having moved Father Benito's things into his bedroom, he and Florence with the assistance of Josie and Miguel were setting up an office for him in the room nearest to his bedroom. Next, they wanted to furnish a conference room and an administrative assistant's office. Needing a break from their busyness they stopped there.

Father Benito, Hans, the Sisters, Josie, and Miguel had been having breakfast every morning at the café. They frequently interacted with William and his friend, Brian, and his construction crew. Benito observed that William was thriving. He was slimming down, building arm muscles, acquiring a tan, and feeling more confident in himself. He seemed happier, exchanging wise-cracks with his buddies. His buddies had families that traditionally were Catholics as were many of the townspeople. They began to recognize Father Benito and to seek to visit with him at the café. They expressed that they missed having a parish church since it had burned down. Benito, seeking to respond kindly to their feelings of being abandoned, invited them all to the picnic.

At the homestead the group fell into the habit of breaking for a period of mid-morning prayer and recollection followed by refreshments. Benito had asked Rosa to prepare beverages and snacks for them and hired her for her services. She was eager to earn money and agreed, providing that Mari stay with her.

Mari had difficulty adjusting to the situation especially learning to play by herself while her Mommy was busy. Hearing Mari cry and fuss, Benito asked Mari to hold his hand and walk across the courtyard to *Abuela* Irene's home. Mari shyly agreed and clung tightly to his hand. Knocking on Irene's door, Mari hid behind Benito's leg. Irene was delighted to see them. Benito invited Irene to accompany them back to the big house for a "tea party." Peeking around Benito's leg, Mari, hearing those words became curious. Picking up on Benito's game, Irene agreed. Benito, with Mari's help, pushed Irene in her wheelchair up the ramp and to the small kitchen table. Explaining to Rosa that *Abuela* Irene was now ready for their tea party, Benito sat down at the table. Irene, winking at Mari, whispered to her, "Come help me to get a surprise." Wheeling herself over to the china cabinet, Irene opened the flimsy glass door. Mari, wide-eyed, gazed at the delicate pretties inside. Irene gently reached in and picked up a miniature china tea-set painted with pink roses. The tiny tea-pot and two cups were crowded onto a small oval platter. Irene and Mari carried them back to the kitchen table and proceeded to play tea party. Rosa brought them a bowl of fruit cut into small pieces pierced with toothpicks. After about an hour, it was obvious that a good time was being had by all. A new mid-morning tradition had been created.

Irene was closely observing Mari, thinking, "This little child seems so hesitant. Even fearful. She constantly looks at her mother as if afraid to lose sight of her. This doesn't seem quite right." When Rosa paused in her snack preparations, Irene motioned for her to come and sit beside her. Irene asked her, "What is your story Rosa? And Mari's?" Rosa looked at her suspiciously. Irene noticed that Rosa too seemed fearful.

Irene remained silent handing tea cups back and forth with Mari. Rosa said, "Thank you for playing with her. Usually, she won't play with anyone. She seems to like you though. Mari? Do you like *Abuela* Irene?" Mari nodded her head yes, walked close to Irene and bending, laid her head in Irene's lap holding it there while quietly smiling at her Mommy. Irene hesitantly reached her shaky hand out and laid it gently on Mari's head, holding it there, quietly. Rosa could see that Mari was relaxing and beginning to close her eyes and indicated that to Irene. Looking around, Irene motioned to Sister Florence who also assessed Mari's need for a nap. Florence found a folded cot, soft blanket, and pillow. She and Rosa set up a napping corner near the china cabinet while Benito picked up Mari, gently carried her, and settled her down into the snuggly nest for a nap.

Irene felt a gentleness settle over her like a velvet cloak being draped around her shoulders. She asked Rosa if she would push her in the wheelchair back to the cottage. Rosa deftly negotiated the ramp and driveway and Irene let herself through her front door. Thanking Rosa, Irene said in parting, "Oh, and tomorrow could you bring some of Mari's toys that we could play with?" Rosa looked at the floor in silence. Irene thought, *Uh oh.* She said to Rosa, "Do you think that Mari might need a few new toys?" Rosa smiled gratefully at Irene and with a light step returned to her kitchen domain. Irene laughed at herself, *Yes, you are! You are hooked on that child, you old Grandma!*

Over the next week everyone was having fun turning the farmhouse into their play-house. Benito and Florence converted the second living room or den into a chapel. They asked Diego if he would place his hand carved statue of Our Lady of Guadalupe at the front of the chapel, "for everyone's inspiration." He proudly agreed and worked diligently completing the finishing touches and delicately painting red roses around the base, a golden halo around the head, and the dress blue. He picked fresh wildflowers putting them into a quart fruit-jar in water and placing them at the feet of Our Lady.

With Irene's agreement they setup bedrooms for Rosa and Mari, the two Sisters, Hans, Josie, and Miguel. Father Benito bought a van for Elena and clothes for all the boys, Elena, Rosa, Josie, Miguel, and little Mari.

Benito told the boys that he expected them to enroll in school. It was to begin soon. He asked Miguel to tutor them to prepare them for the new school year. Miguel set up a mini class room in one of the upstairs bedrooms and drew up a daily schedule of attendance for the boys. Benito asked William to setup a construction workshop in the barn with basic power tools and materials. William agreed to give the boys classes and an opportunity to build and work on a project together.

Elena offered her home for the project. It badly needed basic repairs. William was enthusiastic about the assignment. Elena was hovering over the activity until William asked her to let him do the supervising. The boys initially wondered if they should act teenage-resistant at being told what to do. Soon curiosity and their enjoyment in the activities won the day and they eagerly complied with Father Benito's instructions. Their awkwardness gradually transitioned into raised self-esteem turning into pride in their accomplishments. Benito paid them each a small stipend for their construction work. Having their own earned money empowered them to feel grown up.

Sister Gratia and William conferred on ideas, designs, and plans to rebuild the burned down Catholic Church. Gratia and William agreed that the focus of the building should be to express the parish mission: "Our community growing spiritually and building itself." The sanctuary should express the goal: "Grace and Community." They explored how opportunities for that might be afforded by including such features as niches for meditation and private prayer, uplifting architectural beauty, ample space for congregant worship, a plaza with a fountain in the center and a performance riser, conversation corners with comfortable chairs, patio tables, children's play areas, areas for cooking, crafts, exercise, discussion groups, a gathering place of respite for the homeless with food, clothing, cots, child care, laundry facilities, office machines, phones, classes, and on and on.

Gratia engaged William in similar challenges of design and planning for the construction of housing units in St. Louis, a project of her religious order. They both bubbled with energy and excitement as they exchanged ideas.

Father Benito increasingly spent time in the chapel. He was inspired to increase his practice of meditating, listening for spiritual guidance, learning to recognize opportunities for individuals and groups and himself to experience spiritual growth. He was striving to increase his living in a sense of awareness of the Grace of Life flowing everywhere, on its own, as it willed. Sister Florence sought out times of reflection as often as possible soaking up peace and walking in nature. Time moved steadily forward dawning into the morning of the picnic.

CHAPTER TWENTY-THREE-PICNIC

August

The homestead's five acres spread out its shady old trees, freshly mowed green lawn, and clumps of cheerfully blooming wildflowers. The catering company scattered it with groups of lawn chairs, picnic tables, blankets on the grass, beverage stations, and lawn toys, including, horseshoes, croquet, bocce balls, badminton, and an inflated bounce-house. Multi-colored *pinatas* were hanging from the trees. There was a four-wheeler and a riding course for it marked out on the back side of the property behind the barn. A bandstand riser had been built for the band. It was colorfully decorated with large colored paper flowers and streamers. Upon it the Mexican Band was warming up and watching the people begin to arrive. Near the house, tables were lined-up and filled with spicy smelling Tex-Mex food dishes of all kinds, fresh fruits, salads, and desserts. They were manned by smiling apron-clad servers. Elena and Hans were trying to be everywhere completing the final arrangements. Along the driveway the boys had marked off a parking lot on a section of the lawn. They were assisting the guests with the parking of their vehicles.

On the front porch Irene was sitting in her wheelchair with Father Benito standing next to her. She remarked, "Father Benito this is impressive. You have brought this old homestead back to life. Thank you. This is the way a home place should be." Benito smiling said to her thoughtfully, "Irene, I think that this is supposed to be leading to something more. I'm not sure what. What do you think?"

Assuming her practical persona she considered his question. "Well, it's obvious to me that by all these people following you out here, hungry for food, of course, but also hungry for more than just tamales. Why don't you ask them if they want to rebuild the church?" To herself she said *You already know the answer to that, don't you, Irene Smith? And, maybe you would like to have a women's Sunday school class started, too, right?* She smiled to herself and wondered how long it would take for this good-hearted pastor to catch on to what he was really wanting as well.

The people kept pouring in. One hundred, two hundred, three hundred. The band, energized, played lively songs that people couldn't help but sing and dance to, laughing, and moving in time to the music. The teenagers were racing the four-wheelers around the track whooping and hollering to each other to, "Go faster!" The little kids were jumping up and down, falling on purpose, squealing in fun, rocking the bounce house. All ages were playing the lawn games challenging and teasing each other.

Irene was joined on the porch by two old men. They reminisced, telling stories about all the people they used to know and the fun things that had happened in their lives. The food was eaten with great appreciation. Eventually, people slowed down and relaxed comfortably on the lawn. A group of men approached Father Benito. Everyone watched them, whispering to each other in expectation. They consulted with him, occasionally raising an arm for emphasis. One of the men, with the agreement of all the others, stepped upon the band's riser taking the microphone while the band members sat silently.

"As most of you know me, my introduction will be brief. I am James Patrick Murphy. I run the auto parts store in town. Anyway, a lot of us from around here remember Father Benito when we had a Catholic Church before it burned down. Well, we just spelled it out to him that we miss having our church, and him, even if his sermons did sometimes run past the beginning of the Sunday noon Cowboys' football game. (Chuckles).

We asked him if he would reopen the church here in our town. So, now, what do you all think? Do you want Father Benito to start our church again?" Patrick looked at the crowd and spread his arms open to them. A few isolated Yeses were heard. Then more and more until the crowd was standing and chanting "Yes!" Patrick closed his arms, turned his clasped hands towards Father Benito and climbed down off the riser. Benito climbed up taking his place. Smiling at them he said kindly, "I understand that you have missed having your parish church and want it back. You know that only the archbishop can authorize that of course. If you wish for me to ask him for you, I will. We'll see what he says.

"As far as me being re-appointed as your pastor, if that were possible, *I would like for us to make some important adaptations moving forward and not be weighed down by some of the old ways that hold us back from growing spiritually. I feel called to point us to grow spiritually in the direction of more kindness to each other, to take more seriously, and even urgently, Jesus's teaching of 'doing unto others as you would have them do unto you.' Recalling dear Jesus' words in response to his disciple's question as to how they could love God, he replied, 'How can you love the Father who you cannot see when you do not love your neighbor, who you can see?'*

"So, I humbly caution you to 'Be careful what you are asking for because you might get it.' And, when we ask to be led to grow spiritually, it can involve change and even turn our lives upside down. I know. I am speaking from experience. But if that's what we want as a community, I can assure you that the Grace will come to move us forward in growing in the knowledge and love of God. And it will bring wonderful joy and happiness into our lives.

"And, I sincerely thank you for expressing that you would like for me to be your pastor. Thank you." Benito spread out his arms, closed his eyes, and waved the sign of the cross over them.

Satisfied and smiling, some of the people began leaving making their way past the servers, Irene, and Father Benito, expressing their thankyous. Many of the people lingered, enjoying visiting with each other in this pleasant setting and drinking after-dinner coffees. It reminded them of their former country farm homes where they grew up.

Stepping out of the peaceful lull, Rosa came up to Irene asking, "Would you come help Mari with her first *piñata*?" Agreeing, Rosa pushed Irene in her wheel chair across the grass. Mari, looking worried, was sitting very still and quiet on the blanket on the ground where her Mommy had left her. Seeing

153

Mommy and Irene approaching, she jumped up and ran to them. She immediately climbed into Irene's lap and clung to her blouse. Rosa spoke softly to Mari, "Mari, *Abuela* Irene is going to help you with your *piñata*. It will be fun." Irene smiled and softly laughed engaging the uncertain child. Rosa handed a wooden broom handle to Irene who picked up Mari's hands and gently fitted her little fingers around it then covered them with her own old wrinkled hands. Grinning and giggling, Irene and Mari began slowly swinging the stick at the *piñata* dangling from the tree. Deliberately missing it several times, Irene asked Mari, "Do you think that we can hit it and break it open next time?" Mari grinned and said "Yes." in a slightly raised voice. Irene said in an excited voice, "Here we go, Mari! Swing! Swing! Swing!" They made contact, ripping open the paper figure, and scattering the contents of candy everywhere. Mari jumped down off of Irene's lap, laughing and scooping up as much candy as her small hands could hold. Irene and Rosa enjoyed Mari as much, or maybe more, than Mari enjoyed the bonanza of her first *piñata*. With both hands full, Mari climbed back up into Irene's lap, smiling happily, showing off her treasures.

From among the small crowd that had gathered around them watching the fun, one of the older men that had been visiting with Irene on the front porch a bit earlier, stepped forward. Seeking Irene's personal attention, he attempted to make a joke by saying to her with a smirk, "Well, that was something. Now, I guess you'll have to go de-bug yourself from holding that greasy little *Mesican* wetback, won't you?" He laughed sarcastically, looking around at the others, but especially at Irene, to watch her and the onlookers admire his wit and laugh with him at his joke.

Irene's face fell. Her heart flinched from the stinging racist cruelty of his hatred, splashed like acid, unfeelingly, upon this precious and innocent child. And upon her mommy, who began tearing up. Irene hugged Mari close to her while Rosa pushed them towards the house. Within Irene's stunned state, she was buried in the suffocating thought that she herself had done the same awful thing to Mari's old *Abuela* who was on her knees and caught up in her childlike innocence, in an ecstasy of anticipation of receiving her beloved Lord in Holy Communion. Irene softly cried, praying, "O Lord, please forgive us! Please forgive us all."

Needing a few days of rest following the flurry of the picnic project, everyone slipped back into their routines. During their mid-morning break, they shared their stories of their journeys of migration. They also began to discuss their individual future plans.

The Sisters were making plans to return to their missions while Hans was servicing his Hummer.

Father Benito telephoned the Archbishop's assistant and conveyed the community's request for the reestablishment of the local parish. Benito was in touch with his USCCB office in Washington, D.C. and they were agreeing to support his decisions regarding his current efforts to assist local immigrants with their migrant problems.

Sister Gratia invited Miguel to travel with her to explore taking a teaching assistant position. She thought that they might be able to secure a teaching visa for him. Sister Gratia reflected, "I am feeling a strong need to record the events and messages of the Showings of Our Lady of Guadalupe's revelations to me while Father Benito was on the ghost mountain, La Place de las Animas. I am thinking that it will take the form of a book of meditative reflections. We'll see what happens with it."

Josie said that she wanted a visa to be able to safely stay in the U.S. Or failing that, she wanted to return to Mexico to avoid being jailed indefinitely.

Rosa admitted that she lived in fear of being discovered and arrested and was constantly terrified that Mari would be taken away from her again. She was afraid to go out among people and try to find work to support herself. She wanted to run, to hide, and to keep moving on.

Elena wondered if the boys were legal and would be allowed

to stay with her and attend school. She didn't know about her own legal status and felt unsure about her safety. She had been working for cash, cleaning peoples' homes and performing personal care services for the ill and elderly. She was earning very little money and often went hungry and without utilities at times. She didn't know who owned the house that she was living in, as she had just sneaked into it one night with her family, and had continued staying there hoping that no one would come by and evict them.

Hearing their accounts of their living circumstances, Irene was shocked. She couldn't imagine how upsetting it must be for them to live with such uncertainties and stresses of being forcibly separated from their family members, being fearful of being arrested, without money or income, and being homeless. Her heart ached for Mari's sense of safety and security. Their feelings of desperation seemed overwhelming.

Following supper, the group retired to the front porch with their hot coffees and teas. This evening, William and Brian drove up in the 'tuff' red pick-up with its dusty silver- knobbed toolbox in the back bed. Leaning out of the driver's side window, Brian, with William at his elbow, grinned at Benito and tempted him to "Meet us at the church construction site tomorrow morning at ten!" Gunning the big motor twice, they drove off laughing into the sunset.

Hans drove Benito and the Sisters to the church site the next morning. Waiting for them was Elena sitting in her van smiling. The sliding side doors opened spilling out the enthusiastic boys. Juan enthused to Benito, "Look Father, we cleaned it all up! Brian and William and their crew used their front-end-loader tractor to scoop up the broken slabs of concrete and beams. It took about twenty loads in their dump truck to get it all removed. We boys worked really hard cleaning up the rest of the smaller parts of the trash. It took us a long time. But we all did it! What do you think about how it looks now?"

Benito, Hans, and the Sisters climbed out of the hummer, walked around the empty site, inspecting where the foundation had been. Smiling, they expressed amazement at the difference the men and boys had made. "It looks great!" Benito declared. "It looks like we will *have* to rebuild the church now!"

James Patrick Murphy and several other men, former parishioners, arrived in their pick-ups. They grew energized and shook hands with Brian and William thanking them and congratulating them on their "Good work!" Approaching Benito, the men spoke all at once questioning, "When can we begin the rebuilding? Did you ask the archbishop yet? What did he say?" William announced, "I'm working on the architectural designs and next up are the blueprints." Following Benito back to the hummer, Patrick spoke to Benito in his business voice, "Father, if you open a Church Building Fund account at the bank, I 'betcha' we can start filling it up." Benito responded positively, "Good idea, Patrick. I'll see what the archbishop thinks about that."

Back at the homestead Benito sat at his office desk, opened the top drawer and took out a yellow legal pad of paper. He lifted his black pen and began writing "Reopening of the Parish of Our Lady of Guadalupe." He took out another yellow legal pad, lifted his pen and entitled the first page, "The Establishment of Our *Abuela* Lady of Guadalupe Shelter for Migrants.

Benito glanced towards the carved statue in the chapel and thought to himself, *Unless the Lord build the house, they labor in vain who build it.* He hoped that the Lord was handing out tool belts to all his saints.

157

CHAPTER TWENTY-FOUR-BUILDERS AT WORK

September

And, so it happened.

With the archbishop's full support, they embarked on the building projects. To celebrate the re-opening of the parish, Benito, the Sisters, Hans, with the newly appointed parish priest, Pastor Father Gomez, joined Patrick's Parish Committee, along with Elena, Juan and the boys, the illegal immigrants and William and his crew. Many former parishioners, including the Hispanic congregants, the remaining old-timers, Buck with his Mom and Dad, and many of his fellow workers from the United Plant Company, all were part of the gathering. Their "Building Anew Mass" was held outdoors on the newly cleared church site. A festive pot-luck picnic was planned to follow.

On the day of the Mass, Father Gomez handed Benito an official Archdiocesan Letter.

Withdrawing privately to the shade of a large sycamore tree, Benito opened it. It was a personal handwritten note from the archbishop. He thanked Benito for his interest and caring about the asylum seekers and immigrants that were struggling within the geographic areas under the archdiocesan jurisdiction.

The archbishop shared that his own grandparents were illegal immigrants and had suffered greatly. He told Benito that a ministry to immigrants was critically important and necessary, therefore, he wanted Benito to not use "development resources" from his Chicago Family. Rather, he wanted the two of them to raise the required funds locally from those who wanted and needed to contribute "whatever it takes" to serve our suffering brothers and sisters in Christ.

The archbishop congratulated him on the re-opening of the parish and stated that he was looking forward to the future successful service to "their" flock.

To Benito's astonishment, the archbishop next stated:

"Due to your zeal in *dearly loving* our brothers and sisters who are desperately migrating, *just to live,* I humbly ask that you accept my appointment to the newly created archdiocesan position of *At Large Auxiliary Bishop* serving the needs of our large population of migrants.

He signed off with "Your Brother in Christ."

Gratitude swelled Father Benito's heart. He happily placed the letter on the altar silently telling the archbishop, "Thank you."

Sitting up front in the first-row area nearest to the temporary altar, in her shiny polished wheelchair, was Irene. She was wearing an old-fashioned large flowered hat.

With Irene was Mari in her modern bright pink dress with large puffed sleeves and a tall stiff pink satin bow topping her long soft black hair. Her small ears sparkled with tiny bright red earrings. Smiling happily, *Abuela* Irene tightly held onto her new "Granddaughter" who was sitting in her lap.

Juan on his knees, with eyes closed, tilted his head heavenward to Our Lady of Guadalupe. He prayed, "Guide me to find and *bust out* our Kids, Mothers, Dads, Brothers, Sisters, and Abuelas."

Juan knew that, again, he would soon set off on a journey to do just that. He added to Our Lady,

"Tell them that we haven't forgotten them. Tell them not to give up. And tell them that *they are dearly loved* and that we will keep lighting candles for them until they are free.

THE END

ABOUT THE AUTHOR

Margaret Malone resides in Oklahoma where she writes, gardens, participates in poetry groups, and votes. Following her service as Sister in the community of the Benedictine Sisters of St. Joseph's Monastery, Tulsa, OK, she married and has two children. She is retired from a career in Social Work and as an Instructor at St. Gregory's University, Shawnee, OK.

Margaret Jane Fletcher Malone (Peggy) earned a B.A. degree in History from Mt. St. Scholastica College, Atchison, KS, a M.S.W. from West Virginia University, Morgantown, W.V., and a Ph.D. in Education from the University of Oklahoma, Norman, OK.

UPCOMING BOOK
BY MAGARET FLETCHER MALONE

SHOWINGS TO SISTER GRATIA
Our Lady of Guadalupe's revelations and teachings to Sister Gratia during Father Benito's experience of "Awakening" while he was spiritually transported to La Place De Las Animas, Ghost Mountain, in the book, DESPERATE TRAVELERS.

Published by Well Being Publishing Company, Oklahoma
welbeco@gmail.com

Made in the USA
Lexington, KY
21 April 2019